CINESTORY COMIC

JOE BOOKS LTD

Published simultaneously in the United States and Canada by Joe Books Ltd,
489 College Street, Suite 203, Toronto, ON M6G 1A5

www.joebooks.com

First Joe Books edition: July 2017

Print ISBN: 978-1-77275-487-2
ebook ISBN: 978-1-77275-790-3

Library and Archives Canada Cataloguing in Publication
information is available upon request.

Printed and bound in Canada
1 3 5 7 9 10 8 6 4 2

OKAY, HERE WE GO. FOCUS.

SPEED.
I AM SPEED.

ONE WINNER. FORTY-TWO LOSERS. I EAT LOSERS FOR BREAKFAST.
DID I USED TO SAY THAT?!

YES, SIR, YA DID.
SHOOT, YOU USED TO SAY THAT ALL THE TIME.
AIGH! MATER!

MATER! WHAT ARE YOU DOING IN HERE?!

WELL, I DIDN'T WANT YA TO BE LONELY.

WELL, THANK YOU. BUT I'M KINDA PREPARING FOR A RACE. I NEED A LITTLE QUIET.
OH, RIGHT!
YOU GOT IT, BUDDY!

HEY, EVERYBODY, LISTEN UP! MY BEST FRIEND, LIGHTNING MCQUEEN, NEEDS QUIET! PERFECT QUIET!

HEH-HEH.
OKAY. WHERE WAS I? RACING. REAL RACING.

HA! THAT AIN'T RACING. THAT WASN'T EVEN A SUNDAY DRIVE. THAT WAS ONE LAP. RACING IS 500 OF THOSE.
EVERYBODY FIGHTING TO MOVE UP LAP AFTER LAP-- INSIDE, OUTSIDE, INCHES APART, NEVER TOUCHING. NOW *THAT'S* RACIN'!
"WELL, I CAN'T ARGUE WITH *THE* DOC HUDSON."
HOW TRUE, HOW TRUE. HA-HAH!

"HEY, LIGHTNING! YOU READY?"

THE FLORIDA INTERNATIONAL SUPER SPEEDWAY.
"OH YEAH. LIGHTNING'S READY. THIS ONE'S FOR YOU, DOC."

SALLY AND THE RADIATOR SPRINGS GANG WATCH LIGHTNING FROM THE PITS.
WOO-HOO! COME ON, STICKERS!
OUTH

'SCUSE ME...PARDON ME...BEST FRIEND COMIN' THROUGH!

GO, MCQUEEN! WOO-HOO!

LIGHTNING MCQUEEN!!!
GO, LIGHTNING! YOU CAN DO IT!

GO, "#95"! WOO-HOO!
LIGHTNING McQUEEN'S BIGGEST FAN!

HEY, CAL, YOUR BLINKER'S ON!

WHAT? NO, IT'S...

...HEY!...YOUR BLINKER'S ON.

GOOD COMEBACK, CAL.

MOTOR SPEEDWAY
FWOOOM

"AND INTO THE PIT GOES LIGHTNING MCQUEEN, BOBBY SWIFT, AND CAL WEATHERS. THESE THREE ARE FUN TO WATCH, AREN'T THEY, DARRELL?"
"YOU KNOW, BOB, I CAN'T TELL IF THEY HAVE MORE FUN ON OR OFF THE TRACK!"
MOTOR SPEEDWAY

FINITO! VIA! VIA! VIA, VIA!

YOU GETTIN' A CAR WASH TOO, CAL?!

NO, *YOU'RE* GETTIN' A CAR WASH, MCQUEEN!!!
GOOD COMEBACK, CAL.

LIGHTNING RACES TO THE FINISH LINE. ANOTHER WIN!

LIGHTNING, HOW DO YOU KEEP YOUR FOCUS RACING AGAINST BOBBY AND CAL?
95

I MEAN, I THINK THE KEY IS WE RESPECT EACH OTHER. THESE GUYS ARE REAL CLASS ACTS...
95

LIVE
AFTER RACE COVERAGE
DINOCO LIGHT 350
CONGRATULATIONS, CUPCAKE! HA-HA-HAH!
HA-HAH!
OH, THEY'RE GONNA PAY.
SPLUTT!
95

CAL AND LIGHTNING ARE LOCKED IN ANOTHER TIGHT FINISH AT THE BIG HEARTLAND MOTOR SPEEDWAY.

DINOCO

GREAT WIN TODAY, CAL.

THANK YOU, SHANNON--
--IT WAS...A GREAT BOOST--
SCREECH!

--AND I'D LIKE...

...HEY. *HEY!!!* GUIDO!

PIT STOP.
HA-HA. LAUGH IT UP. REAL FUNNY.

BACK AT WILLYS BUTTE IN RADIATOR SPRINGS, LIGHTNING TAKES A FAST TRAINING RUN.

KEEP IT GOING, BUDDY!
ANDIAMO!
SPEED
YOUR SPEED

WOO!

STOP WINNING, FOR CRYING OUT LOUD. WE'RE RUNNING OUT OF BUMPER CREAM TO SELL!
HEY! ARE MY SPONSORS HAPPY TODAY?
HA-HAH!

LIGHTNING MCQUEEN!
HEY, BIG TEX! HOW'S MY FAVORITE COMPETITOR?

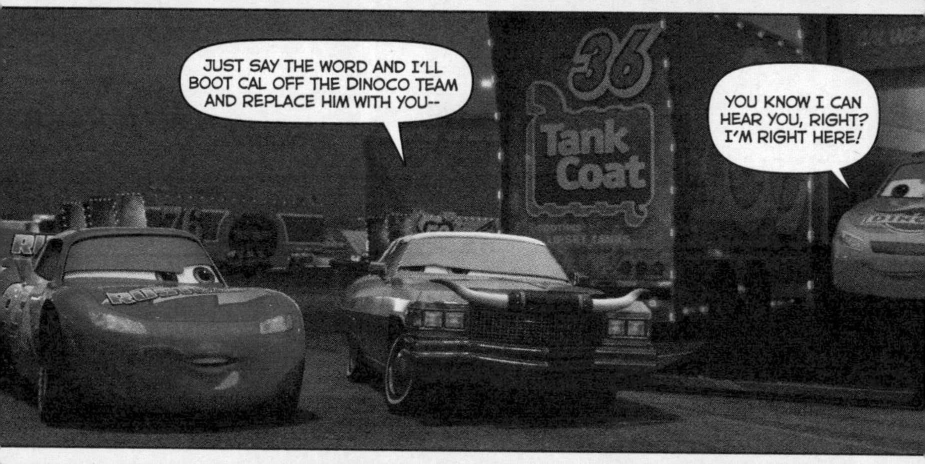
JUST SAY THE WORD AND I'LL BOOT CAL OFF THE DINOCO TEAM AND REPLACE HIM WITH YOU--
YOU KNOW I CAN HEAR YOU, RIGHT? I'M RIGHT HERE!
Tank Coat

BYE, CAL! SEE YOU NEXT WEEK ...OR NOT!
OH, COME ON NOW, I'M JOKING!

GO, LITTLE BUDDY!
WOO-HOO!

AND BIG BUDDY, TOO!

"ANOTHER GREAT FINISH IN THE MAKING! MCQUEEN AND SWIFT, NOSE TO NOSE."

HOW'S THE VIEW BACK THERE, BOBBY?
HA-HA! WELL, YOU BETTER NOT BLINK, I'LL BLOW RIGHT PAST YA!

"THE FLAG IS OUT! IT'S THE FINAL STRETCH! MCQUEEN IS IN THE LEAD..."
OKAY, LET'S SEE WHAT YOU GOT!

"HOLY COW!"
"OH MY!"

"...IT'S JACKSON STORM FOR THE *WIN!* A HUGE UPSET!"
"NEITHER LIGHTNIN' OR BOBBY EVER SAW HIM COMIN'!"

IT'S ONE THING TO START FAST, BUT WE HAVEN'T SEEN ANYONE CROSS THE LINE WITH THAT KIND OF SPEED AND POWER SINCE LIGHTNING MCQUEEN FIRST ARRIVED ON THE SCENE.

JACKSON STORM! HEY, JACKSON! THAT WAS INCREDIBLE! AWESOME! GIVE ME A FEW WORDS! GIVE US A QUOTE! CAN WE GET A PICTURE HERE?
THANK YOU, GUYS. THANK YOU. NO--I APPRECIATE IT. THANK YOU VERY MUCH. THANK YOU.

HEY, JACKSON STORM, RIGHT? GREAT RACE TODAY.

WOW! THANK YOU, MR. MCQUEEN. YOU HAVE NO IDEA WHAT A PLEASURE IT IS FOR ME TO FINALLY BEAT YOU.

OH, THANKS!

WAIT. HANG ON...DID YOU SAY "MEET" OR "BEAT?"

I THINK YOU HEARD ME.
UHH, WHAT?

MCQUEEN! STORM! OVER HERE! CAN WE GET SOME PICTURES?

YEAH, YEAH, COME ON. LET'S GET A PICTURE!

YOU KNOW WHAT, GET A TON OF PICTURES! BECAUSE CHAMP HERE HAS BEEN A ROLE MODEL OF MINE FOR YEARS NOW! AND I MEAN A *LOT* OF YEARS! RIGHT? I LOVE THIS GUY!

OVER HERE! GUYS! THIS WAY! JACKSON! JACKSON! JACKSON STORM! HEY, JACKSON!
JUST A QUOTE! GIVE ME A FEW WORDS! THAT WAS AMAZING!

I THINK I TOUCHED A NERVE.

CHICK'S PICKS
CHICK HICKS
FORMER AND FOREVER
PISTON CUP CHAMPION
WELCOME BACK TO *CHICK'S PICKS* WITH CHICK HICKS!
I'M YOUR HOST, FORMER-AND-FOREVER PISTON CUP CHAMPION CHICK HICKS...DOOT DOOT DOOT DO!

THIS JUST IN--ROOKIE JACKSON STORM SLAMS THE PROVERBIAL DOOR ON LIGHTNING MCQUEEN. OOOOH...I COULDN'T HAVE ENJOYED IT MORE IF I'D BEATEN MCQUEEN MYSELF. OH, WAIT, I HAVE!

BUT ENOUGH ABOUT ME. HERE TO TELL YOU HOW IT HAPPENED IS PROFESSIONAL NUMBER CRUNCHER...

...MISS NATALIE CERTAIN!

IT'S A PLEASURE TO BE HERE, CHICK. AND ACTUALLY, I PREFER THE TERM "STATISTICAL ANALYST."

RIGHT. SO...WHO IS THIS MYSTERIOUS NEWCOMER JACKSON STORM, AND WHY IS HE SO DARN FAST?

ADVANCED SIMUL TRAINING
HYDRO-FORME CHASSIS
CARBO CERAMIC BRA
IT'S NO MYSTERY IF YOU STUDY THE DATA, MR. HICKS. JACKSON STORM IS PART OF THE NEXT GENERATION OF HIGH-TECH RACERS. UNLIKE THE VETERANS OF YESTERDAY--

--STORM ACHIEVES HIS TOP SPEEDS BY EXPLOITING THE NUMBERS.
AVERAGE SPEED: 210.364 MPH

I REFER OF COURSE TO RACING DATA. TIRE PRESSURE, DOWN FORCE, WEIGHT DISTRIBUTION, AERODYNAMICS--
--AND NEXT GENS LIKE STORM ARE TAKING ADVANTAGE. THE RACING WORLD IS CHANGING.

AND FOR THE BETTER IF IT MEANS MY OLD PAL LIGHTNING IS DOWN FOR THE COUNT, AM I RIGHT, CERTAIN?
WELL, IF I'M CERTAIN OF ANYTHING, CHICK, IT'S THAT THIS SEASON IS ABOUT TO GET EVEN MORE INTERESTING.
86

GRANDOL

"I'LL TELL YOU WHAT, DARRELL, JACKSON STORM HAS CERTAINLY MADE AN IMPACT...
"...WE'VE GOT SIX MORE NEXT-GENERATION ROOKIES IN THE FIELD..."

"...WITH SIX VETERANS FIRED TO CLEAR THE WAY."

MORNING, CHAMP. HOW'S OUR "LIVING LEGEND" TODAY?
UH--STILL VERY MUCH ALIVE, THANK YOU, AND I WOULD APPRECIATE--

YOU KNOW, I CAN'T BELIEVE I GET TO RACE *THE* LIGHTNING MCQUEEN IN HIS FAREWELL SEASON.
WHAT ARE YOU TALKING ABOUT?
OOPS, GREEN FLAG--GOOD LUCK OUT THERE, CHAMP! YOU'RE GONNA NEED IT.

CONSTANT TURN RADIUS
ONE REASON STORM AND THE NEXT GENS ARE MORE EFFICIENT? THEIR ABILITY TO HOLD THE OPTIMUM RACING LINE EVERY SINGLE LAP.

MPH
208
STORM'S IN A CLASS OF HIS OWN, AND A BIG REASON FOR THAT? TRAINING ON THE NEWEST, CUTTING-EDGE SIMULATORS. THESE MACHINES CREATE A VIRTUAL RACING EXPERIENCE SO REAL, RACERS NEVER EVEN HAVE TO GO OUTSIDE.

A FRUSTRATED MCQUEEN COMES OUT OF THE TURN AND WHIPS PAST MATER...

"STORM'S ABILITY TO HOLD THAT LINE IS LIKE NOTHING WE'VE EVER SEEN."

"FOUR IN A ROW! ARE YOU KIDDING ME?!"

...TWO PERCENT LOWER DRAG COEFFICIENT...
20

"OH, WHAT A FINISH!"
OFFICIAL

...FIVE PERCENT INCREASED DOWN FORCE...
"LUCKY NUMBER SEVEN!"

...ONE-POINT-TWO PERCENT HIGHER TOP SPEED.
210 MPH
20

"AMAZING! NINE!"

NO, NO, NO, CHICK. MCQUEEN IS A CRAFTY VETERAN CHAMP. HE'S *THE* ELDER STATESMAN OF THE SPORT, YA KNOW?

TAKES EVERYTHING I GOT TO BEAT HIM.

RUSTY AND DUSTY! HEY, TEAM RUST-EZE! TEAM #95!
...WHAT CHANGES ARE YOU GOING TO MAKE TO GET MCQUEEN BACK ON TOP?
...WILL MCQUEEN TRY NEW TRAINING METHODS?
...IS HE PREPARED TO RETIRE?
UH...
COME ON, COME ON, GUYS, LET'S NOT OVERREACT. IT'S JUST A SLUMP. WE'LL GET 'EM NEXT WEEK.

IGHTNING! OVER HERE! Y, MCQUEEN! MCQUEEN!
OKAY, THAT'S ENOUGH. NO COMMENT.
NOT EVEN ABOUT AL WEATHERS RETIRING?

WAIT, WHAT?
L WEATHERS. 'S HANGING UP LIGHTYEARS.

NO. NO COMMENT ON THAT, EITHER.

HEY, CAL? HEY! RETIREMENT? WHAT'S GOING ON?

YOU KNOW, I ASKED MY UNCLE ONCE HOW I'D KNOW WHEN IT WAS TIME TO STOP. YA KNOW WHAT HE SAID? "THE YOUNGSTERS'LL TELL YA."

WE HAD SOME GOOD TIMES TOGETHER. I'M GONNA MISS THAT THE MOST, I THINK.

YEAH.

MORE CHANGES AHEAD, CHICK.

EVERY WEEK WE'VE SEEN VETERAN RACERS EITHER RETIRE-- LIKE CAL WEATHERS TONIGHT--OR BE FIRED TO MAKE ROOM FOR THESE YOUNGER, FASTER RACERS.

AND IT'S NOT OVER YET.

HELLO, RACING FANS. WELCOME TO THE LOS ANGELES 500! FINAL RACE OF THE PISTON CUP SEASON!
IT'S BEEN A YEAR OF SURPRISES AND TODAY PROMISES TO BE NO DIFFERENT. AS THE TEAMS GET READY IN THE PITS, WE GET READY TO BRING YOU THE ACTION HERE TRACKSIDE...
MOTOR SPEEDWAY of the SOUTH

LIGHTNING HEADS TOWARD BOBBY'S GARAGE...
YOU CAN'T DO THIS! I'VE RACED FOR YOU GUYS ALMOST TEN YEARS!
BRICK?

SORRY, BRICK. MY MIND'S MADE UP. I'M GIVING YOUR NUMBER TO SOMEONE NEW.
THE WHOLE SPORT'S CHANGING. I'M JUST DOING WHAT I GOTTA DO...
HEY! I-I HAD TWO WINS LAST YEAR!

HEY, BOBBY? DO YOU KNOW WHAT'S HAPPENING WITH BRICK?

OH...WAIT, YOU'RE NOT BOBBY.

THE NAME'S DANNY, BRO.

"BOOGITY, BOOGITY, BOOGITY! LET'S END THIS SEASON WITH A GREAT RACE!"

HEY, CHAMP...WHERE'D ALL YOUR FRIENDS GO?

THAT'S IT, BUDDY!

"FORTY LAPS TO GO AND RACE LEADER JACKSON STORM IS MAKING HIS WAY ONTO PIT ROAD, WITH MCQUEEN ON HIS TAIL."

"A GOOD STOP HERE COULD MEAN THE DIFFERENCE BETWEEN VICTORY AND DEFEAT."
C'MON, C'MON, C'MON! C'MON!!!
FASTER, GUIDO! C'MON, I GOTTA GET BACK OUT THERE BEFORE HE DOES!

"WHAT A PIT STOP BY MCQUEEN! MAN! HE JUST GOT THE LEAD!"

"BUT DARRELL, CAN HE HOLD ON TO IT?"
HEY, MCQUEEN. YOU ALL RIGHT? LISTEN, DON'T YOU WORRY, PAL. YOU HAD A GOOD RUN. ENJOY YOUR RETIREMENT.
PANT

"STORM TAKES BACK THE LEAD!"

"UNBELIEVABLE! MCQUEEN IS FADING.
MCQUEEN IS FADING...FADING FAST..."

NO! NO, NO, NO, NO!

EERRRT!

WRRTTT!

BLAM!

GASP

BOOOM!

SCREEET!

IT IS THE WORST CRASH OF
LIGHTNING MCQUEEN'S CAREER.
95

FSSSSS...

WEEE-OOo!
WEEE-OOo!
WEEE-OOo!

FOUR MONTHS LATER.
"WELCOME BACK TO *PISTON CUP TALK 'ROUND THE CLOCK,* WHERE WE DO NOTHING BUT TALK RACING. SO LET'S GET TO IT...

"...STARTING OF COURSE WITH LIGHTNING MCQUEEN.
FABULOUS HUDSON HORNET

"WITH THE SEASON START JUST TWO WEEKS AWAY, THERE'S STILL NO OFFICIAL ANNOUNCEMENT, BUT WITH "#95" COMING OFF HIS WORST YEAR ON RECORD, DON'T SHOOT THE MESSENGER HERE, FOLKS...
SPRINGS
BRIC-A-BRAC
U WANT IT WE GOT IT
RARE H
SALE TODAY ONLY
SERVICE
ROUTE 66
"...I THINK IT'S SAFE TO ASSUME THAT LIGHTNING MCQUEEN'S RACING DAYS ARE OVER. MEANWHILE, JACKSON STORM IS LOOKING EVEN FASTER THAN--"

AS THEY ENTER THE FINAL LAP, THE "#6" AND "#12" CARS ARE STILL FIGHTING IT OUT FOR THE LEAD.

BUT WAIT! HERE HE COMES! IT'S THE FABULOUS HUDSON HORNET KNOCKING AT THEIR DOOR! WHAT'S HE GOT UP HIS SLEEVE TODAY?
48467

AND THERE IT IS! WITH ONE INCREDIBLE MOVE, HE'S PAST THEM! THE HORNET TAKES THE DECISIVE LEAD! HE'S LEFT THE PACK BEHIND! HIS CREW CHIEF, SMOKEY, IS LOVING IT! IT'S UNBELIEVABLE!
48467

OH NO! HE'S IN TROUBLE! THE HUDSON HORNET HAS LOST CONTROL! THE HUDSON HORNET HAS LOST CONTROL!

WHAT SHOULD HAVE BEEN A SCENE OF JUBILATION HAS TURNED TRAGIC HERE TODAY, FOLKS, AS WE AWAIT NEWS ON THE HUDSON HORNET'S CONDITION.

AFTER SUCH A DEVASTATING CRASH, WE CAN ONLY HOPE THAT THIS RACE TODAY WASN'T HIS LAST.

The Daily Exhaust FINAL
CRASH!
HUDSON HORNET
OUT FOR SEASON
WHEN I FINALLY GOT PUT TOGETHER, I WENT BACK EXPECTING A BIG WELCOME. YOU KNOW WHAT THEY SAID?

The Daily Exhaust FINAL
CRASH!
HUDSON HORNET
OUT FOR SEASON
Season Ender Fender Bender Puts Young Hornet in Garage
"YOU'RE HISTORY." MOVED RIGHT ON TO THE NEXT ROOKIE STANDING IN LINE. THERE WAS A LOT LEFT IN ME I NEVER GOT A CHANCE TO SHOW 'EM.

HEY, STICKERS.
HOW YA FEELING?
WHA--? OH. HEY, SAL.

YEAH. GREAT. REALLY, REALLY GREAT.
THINKING ABOUT DOC AGAIN?
95

YEAH. YOU KNOW, THEY TOLD HIM WHEN HE WAS DONE. HE DIDN'T DECIDE.

SIGH I DON'T WANT WHAT HAPPENED TO DOC TO HAPPEN TO ME.

BUT THAT HASN'T HAPPENED.

NO. BUT I CAN'T GO OUT ON THE TRACK AND DO THE SAME OLD THING--IT WON'T WORK.
THEN CHANGE IT UP. TRY SOMETHING NEW.

I DON'T KNOW, SALLY...
DON'T FEAR FAILURE. BE AFRAID OF NOT HAVING THE CHANCE. YOU HAVE THE CHANCE! DOC DIDN'T.
AND YOU CAN EITHER TAKE IT, OR YOU CAN DO WHAT YA BEEN DOING--SITTIN' IN HERE FOR MONTHS...

...AND BY THE WAY, I LOVE WHAT YOU'VE DONE WITH THE PLACE...
...I MEAN, THE MONSTER-MOVIE LIGHTING AND THE, UH, MUSKY AIR FRESHENER--AND DON'T LET ANYONE TELL YOU YOU'RE NOT WORKING THAT PRIMER BECAUSE, WOW, I HAVE NEVER FOUND YOU MORE ATTRACTIVE.
AND NOW THAT I'VE BEEN IN HERE FOR A COUPLE MINUTES...THE STENCH...I'M GETTING KIND OF USED TO IT!

OKAY, OKAY, SAL, I GET IT. I GET IT.
I MISS YOU, LIGHTNING. WE ALL DO.

TRY SOMETHING NEW, HUH...

HEY--DID IT WORK, MISS SALLY?! DID YOU SET HIM STRAIGHT WITH YOUR LAWYERLY POWERS OF PERSUASION?
IS HE READY TO START TRAININ'?

YES, MATER, I AM.
WELL, STINKY--STICKERS?!
I DECIDE WHEN I'M DONE.
I WAS HOPING YOU'D SAY THAT.
WOOOOOOHOOHOOHOO!

OKAY--BUT I'VE GOT AN IDEA, AND I'M GONNA NEED TO TALK TO RUSTY AND DUSTY, ALL RIGHT?

I'LL GET 'EM ON THE HORN! GET IT? "ON THE HORN!" HA-HA-HA!
KEEP OUT
NO TRESPASSING

Flo's
Cafe

WHAT ABOUT THE CAR FROM EVERETT? REMEMBER HIM?
HE WAS STUCK IN REVERSE! I SAID, "YOU NEED A HOUSE WITH A CIRCULAR DRIVEWAY!"

HA-HA-HA! YOU BOYS NEED TO GET YOUR RUSTY TAILS DOWN HERE. I CREATED A DRINK IN YOUR HONOR.
RADIATOR

YEAH! THE RUST-EZE MEDICATED BUMPER BOMB. IT GOES DOWN FASTER THAN AN ELEVATOR FULL OF WINNEBAGOS.

HA-HA-HAH!!!

RUSTY AND DUSTY!
RADIATOR SPRINGS CURIOS

Phone
HEY! THERE HE IS! GOOD TO SEE YOU, LIGHTNING!

THANKS, GUYS! WOW...

...YOU'RE ALL HERE.

SORRY, BUDDY, DID YOU WANT THIS CALL TO BE PRIVATE?

NO, MATER,
THIS IS PERFECT.

LISTEN--THANKS EVERYONE, FOR STICKING BY ME. IT TOOK ME A WHILE TO FIGURE IT OUT...
...BUT I KNOW NOW THAT IT'S TIME FOR ME TO MAKE SOME CHANGES.

CHANGES? WHAT KIND OF CHANGES?
WESTERN
51237

IT'S FUTILE TO RESIST CHANGE, MAN.
51237

YOU'RE RIGHT, FILLMORE.
REALLY?!

WHICH IS WHY I HAVE AN ANNOUNCEMENT TO MAKE.
I'VE THOUGHT LONG AND HARD ABOUT IT...
...DONE A LOT OF SOUL SEARCHING AND CONSIDERED ALL OF THE OPTIONS...
...AND I'VE FINALLY DECIDED...

YOU DO WANT TO KEEP RACING?

ARE YOU KIDDING?! OF COURSE I WANNA KEEP RACING!

THE THING IS, GUYS, IF I'M GONNA BE FASTER THAN STORM, I NEED TO TRAIN LIKE HIM.

WE'RE WAY AHEAD OF YOU, BUDDY!
LIGHTNING, WE WANT YOU ON THE ROAD FIRST THING IN THE MORNING...
...SO YOU CAN COME OUT AND SEE THE BRAND NEW...
...RUST-EEEEEZE RACING CENTER!

IT'S WICKED AWESOME!

WHAT?! RUST-EZE RACING CENTER?

IT'S GOT ALL THE FANCY BELLS AND WHISTLES THAT THE KIDS ARE TRAINING ON THESE DAYS.
WE'LL SEND MACKY BOY ALL THE DIRECTIONS. NOW GET MOVIN', ALL RIGHT?
DODGE

O-OKAY! YES!

RUST-EZE RACING CENTER! WOO-HOO!
FANCY NEW TRAINING CENTE THAT SOUNDS NI
IT'S TIME TO CELEBRATE!

HEY, MCQUEEN! YOU CAN'T RACE IN PRIMER, MAN. COME ON! LET'S GO.
95

Rust-eze
BUMPER OINTMENT
LIGHTYEAR
95
LIGHTYEAR

RAMONE, YOU HAVE DONE IT AGAIN.

IT'S LIKE THE SISTINE CHAPEL--ON WHEELS.

I'M COMING FOR YOU, STORM.

MORNING, MCQUEEN! HEY, LOOK AT YOU.
JUST LIKE YOUR OLD SELF. THAT'S QUITE A SPIT SHINE!
OH! HE LOOKS SO GOOD.
YOU LOOK GREAT, MAN!

WELCOME BACK. YOU LOOK ...DIFFERENT.
OBVIOUSLY.

YOU LOOK READY.

GUIDO, COME! SCUSI, SCUSI. TIRES COMING THROUGH.

GOOD LUCK IN COLLEGE.
ALL RIGHT, BYE!

GO GET 'EM, TIGER! CATCH YA ON THE FLIP SIDE!

I'LL SEE YOU GUYS IN FLORIDA!

DON'T FORGET TO CALL ME!

HEY, SAL, THANKS.

ANYTIME.

LOVE YOU.

LOVE YOU MORE.

GOOD LUCK, MAN! SEE YA LATER, GATER!

RUST-EZE RACING CENTER, HERE WE COME! GOOD TIMES AHEAD! YEEEAH!
MACK

RUSTEZE
RACING CENTER
Lightning McQueen
95

HEY, MCQUEEN! OVER HERE! MCQUEEN, HOW YOU FEELING?

HAVE YOU SEEN THE LATEST RECORDS STORM'S BEEN SETTING?
HAVE YOU GIVEN ANY THOUGHT TO RETIREMENT? MCQUEEN! OVER HERE!

OKAY! THAT'S ENOUGH. NO QUESTIONS! *SCUSI*. OUT OF THE WAY! COMING THROUGH! BACK UP. BACK UP!

SCORRERE, SCORRERE. FATE PASSARE.
HEY, MCQUEEN! OVER HERE! MCQUEEN! MCQUEEN!
NO PICTURES! NO, NO, NO. OKAY, THANK YOU! BUH-BYE!

GUIDO, CAN YOU BELIEVE THEM?
PAPARAZZI PTUI!

OOOOOH! WOW!
LOOKS GOOD, DOESN'T IT?

HEY, GUYS!
WHATTA YA THINK?

WHAT DO I THINK? IT'S UNBELIEVABLE!

GUYS, HOW DID YOU EVER DO THIS?
YEAHHH, YOU KNOW, IT'S KIND OF A COZY, HUMBLE, LITTLE PLACE.
95

YOU WANT TO TELL HIM OR SHOULD I TELL HIM?
AH--YOU START! GO AHEAD, GO AHEAD!
WE SOLD RUST-EZE!
DODGE

WHAT?!

WHAT? YOU THINK A COUPLE OF JABRONIS LIKE US COULD DO THIS ON OUR OWN?
DODGE

WAIT. YOU SOLD RUST-EZE?

IT'S ALL GOOD NEWS.
WE JUST REALIZED YOU NEEDED SOMETHING WE COULDN'T GIVE YOU.
DODGE

IT FELT LIKE THE TIME WAS RIGHT FOR US, TOO. I MEAN, WE'RE NOT AS YOUNG AND HANDSOME AS WE LOOK.
OH, THAT'S TRUE.
BESIDES... THIS STERLING FELLA? HE'S GOT EVERY HIGH-TECH THING YOU'LL *EVER* NEED.
EVERYTHING WE *WANTED* TO GIVE YOU, BUT COULDN'T.
DODGE

WHOA, WHOA, WHOA--STERLING? WHO'S STERLING?
95

LIGHTNING MCQUEEN!
YOU MADE SOME SERIOUS TIME, PARTNER.

YOUR NEW SPONSOR! HE'S THE MUD FLAP KING OF THE EASTERN SEABOARD!

WELCOME TO THE RUST-EZE RACING CENTER! YOU HAVE NO IDEA HOW MUCH I'VE BEEN LOOKING FORWARD TO THIS.
THANKS, UH... MISTER...
PLEASE. NO "MISTER," JUST STERLING. I HAVE BEEN A FAN OF YOURS FOREVER. AND TO BE YOUR SPONSOR? HOW GREAT IS THAT?

I CAN'T THANK RUSTY AND DUSTY HERE ENOUGH. TOUGH NEGOTIATORS, BY THE WAY.
AH. YOU FLATTER US--BUT DON'T STOP!
HA-HA-HA.
PISTON CUP

ANYWAY...JUST WANTED TO SAY A QUICK "HELLO." TAKE AS MUCH TIME AS YOU NEED.
DOOR'S ALWAYS OPEN, GUYS.
DODGE
PISTON CUP

SEE?
DODGE

WELL, I-I SURE AM GONNA MISS RACING FOR YOU GUYS.
95

YA KNOW, YOU GAVE US A LOT OF GREAT MEMORIES, LIGHTNING. MEMORIES WE'LL REMEMBER.
WOW. THAT'S GOOD.

HEY, LIGHTNING, WHATEVER YOU DO, DON'T DRIVE LIKE MY BROTHER.
...DON'T DRIVE LIKE MY BROTHER.

NO, NO, PLEASE. NO PICTURES. OKAY, MAYBE ONE. GET MY GOOD SIDE THOUGH, WILL YA?
HEH-HEH.

WHOA.

SO? YOU LIKE IT?

OH, HEY, MR. STERLING. WOW! MY CAREER ON A WALL. NICE THAT YOU INCLUDED DOC.

Doc Hudson
CREW CHIEF AND MENTOR OF LIGHTNING McQUEEN
OF COURSE. HE WAS YOUR MENTOR...
...LOSING HIM LEFT A GIANT HOLE IN THE SPORT.

YEAH...

...JARS OF DIRT?

SACRED DIRT. EACH OF THOSE JARS CONTAINS DIRT FROM ALL THE OLD TRACKS THAT DOC RACED ON--FLORIDA INTERNATIONAL, THUNDER HOLLOW, JUST DOWN THE ROAD, AND OUR VERY OWN FIREBALL BEACH, RIGHT OUTSIDE.

HUH. HEY, IS THAT--

A BIT OF ASPHALT FROM GLEN ELLEN...
MY FIRST WIN!

YOU REALLY ARE A FAN.
DIRT CLASSIC

I AM. AND A FAN OF YOUR FUTURE.
YOU READY FOR IT?

DEFINITELY.
DIRT CLASSIC

"FIRST LET'S
GET YOU INTO A MORE...
CONTEMPORARY LOOK."
WHOOSH

THUMP THUMP

A NEW BODY WRAP
SEALS INTO PLACE.

WOW!

IT'S AN ELECTRONIC SUIT. WITH IT WE'LL BE ABLE TO TRACK YOUR SPEED AND YOUR VITAL SIGNS.
REALLY?! DOES IT HAVE A PHONE?
DON'T BE CRAZY! RACE CARS DON'T HAVE PHONES!

WOW!

NOT BAD, HUH?
THIS IS REALLY IMPRESSIVE.

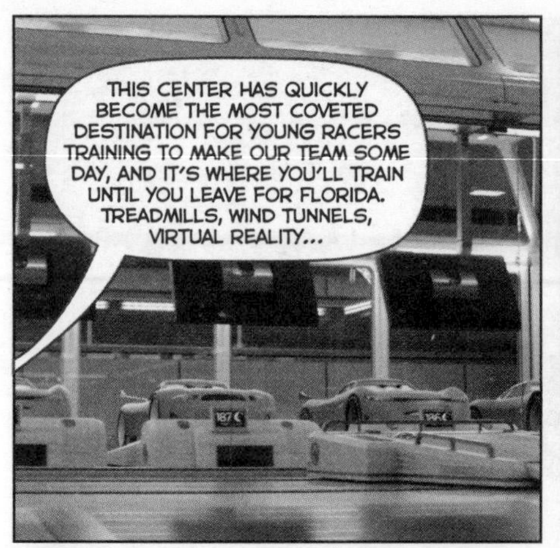
THIS CENTER HAS QUICKLY BECOME THE MOST COVETED DESTINATION FOR YOUNG RACERS TRAINING TO MAKE OUR TEAM SOME DAY, AND IT'S WHERE YOU'LL TRAIN UNTIL YOU LEAVE FOR FLORIDA. TREADMILLS, WIND TUNNELS, VIRTUAL REALITY...

...STILL WORKING ON THAT... AND THE BEST FITNESS REGIMENS ANYONE COULD POSSIBLY IMAGINE--

WAIT. WAIT. HO-HO-HO...IS THAT THE SIMULATOR?

OH, YES. LIGHTNING MCQUEEN, I'D LIKE TO INTRODUCE YOU TO THE MULTIMILLION DOLLAR FLAGSHIP OF INTERACTIVE RACE SIMULATION...

...THE XDL 24-GTS MARK Z.
JACKSON STORM WISHES HE HAD THIS MODEL.
THE XDL-- ETCETERA.

SPEED
188
4
LAP 5 16:23

TOP SPEED
193
3
LAP 5 28:26

TOP SPEED
193
3

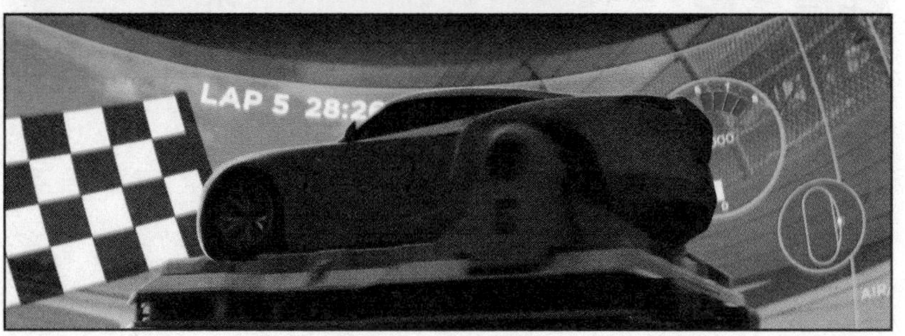

LAP 5

ALL RIGHT! THAT WAS AMAZING! WHOA!
IT'S JUST LIKE BEING ON A REAL TRACK, SO PUT YOUR HOURS IN! OKAY, LET'S HIT THE TREADMILLS! COME ON. SHOW ME WHAT YOU GOT!

WOW. PRETTY FAST. WHO'S THE RACER?

NO, NO, NO, SHE'S NOT A RACER-- SHE'S A TRAINER. CRUZ RAMIREZ, THE BEST TRAINER IN THE BUSINESS.

READY TO "*MEET* IT, *GREET* IT..."

AND DEFEAT IT!

ALL RIGHT, NOW BRING UP THOSE RPMS.

LIKE THE ATTITUDE!
YEAH. WE CALL HER OUR MAESTRO OF MOTIVATION.

YOU'RE DRIVIN' A LITTLE TENSE AGAIN, RONALD.

NO, NO, NO, I'M COOL. I'M COOL.

DO YOUR EXERCISE.

I AM A FLUFFY CLOUD. I AM A FLUFFY CLOUD. I AM A FLUFFY...
153 mph
185

YOU'RE A CLOUD. HA-HAH--
155 mph
188

SHUT UP, KURT!
184
187

KURT! HERE COME THE BUGS, KURT. YOU READY?

187

186

HEY, I KEPT MY EYES OPEN THIS TIME!

GOTTA SEE THAT TRACK!

OH, NO...

142

...HOMESICK AGAIN, GABRIEL?
SI.

SANTA CECILIA! MI PUEBLO!

WIN FOR THEM!
TREADSTER

SHE TRAINS YOUNG RACERS TO PUSH THROUGH THEIR OWN OBSTACLES.
TAILOR MADE FOR EACH ONE.
WOW!
NOW, SHE'S GONNA WORK WITH YOU.

LET'S GO, LET'S GO! YOU GUYS GOTTA WORK THROUGH THIS STUFF SO WHEN YOUR BIG CHANCE COMES ALONG, YOU CAN TAKE IT!
TREADSTER

OH, HEY, MR. STERLING!
HEY, CRUZ!

I'D LIKE TO INTRODUCE YOU TO LIGHTNING MCQUEEN.

I HEAR YOU'RE THE MAESTRO.

MR. STERLING, DID YOU SAY LIGHTNING MCQUEEN WAS HERE, BECAUSE I DON'T SEE HIM ANYWHERE.

UH--BUT HE'S RIGHT HERE. DO YOU NOT SEE HIM?

NOPE. STILL DON'T SEE HIM.

HE'S RIGHT IN FRONT OF YOU. IT'S LIGHTNING MCQUEEN.

HE'S OBVIOUSLY AN IMPOSTER--HE LOOKS OLD AND BROKEN DOWN, WITH FLABBY TIRES!

HEY! I DO NOT!

USE THAT!!!

WHOA! OH. HA-HA-HA. YEAH, I SEE, I CAN USE THAT ENERGY FOR MOTIVATION, RIGHT? RARRR.

IT'S ABOUT MOTIVATION, MR. MCQUEEN. YOU CAN USE ANYTHING NEGATIVE AS FUEL TO PUSH THROUGH TO THE POSITIVE!

BEEN PRETTY POSITIVE, EVER SINCE I WAS A ROOKIE.

I AM SO EXCITED THAT I GET TO TRAIN YOU--I GREW UP WATCHING YOU ON TV.

HUH. IS THAT RIGHT?

THESE YOUNG GUYS ARE GREAT AND ALL, BUT *I* LIKE A CHALLENGE!

HA-HA, I'M NOT THAT MUCH OLDER BUT...

IN FACT, I CALL YOU MY SENIOR PROJECT.

THE NEXT DAY.

WE NEED TO LOOSEN THOSE ANCIENT JOINTS.

FIRST THE WHEELS! AND FORWARD AND REST, AND FORWARD AND REST-- JOIN ME! REST... AND REST...

IS ALL THIS RESTING NECESSARY?
WE'RE WORKING YOU IN SLOWLY.

AND REACH FOR YOUR LUNCH.

WHEN DO I--
REACH FOR YOUR LUNCH. NOW REEEACH--
SHOULDN'T WE BE--
--TO THE FRONT--

--WHAT IS THERE?
I DON'T THINK THIS IS--
IT'S YOUR LUNCH!

NOW BACKWARD! IS LUNCH THERE?!

WHEN DO WE GO ON THE SIMULATOR?

RUSTEZE
AAH!

GOOD MORNING, MR. MCQUEEN. LOOKING GOOD!
AHH! WHY?

THIS'LL GET OIL TO PLACES IT HASN'T BEEN IN A LONG TIME!

IS THAT-- A DRIP PAN?
JUST IN CASE...
RUSTEZE

RUSTEZE
95
HOW OLD DO YOU THINK I AM?

VISUALIZE YOURSELF DRIVING FAST DOWN A STEEP HILL. I'LL BE BACK IN A FEW.

VISUALIZE? WAIT, WAIT! CRUZ!
RUSTEZE
95

A FEW WHAT?!
RUSTEZE
95

I JUST WANT TO GO ON THE SIMULATOR...
HOW'S IT HANGING, DRIP PAN?
RUSTEZE
95

012

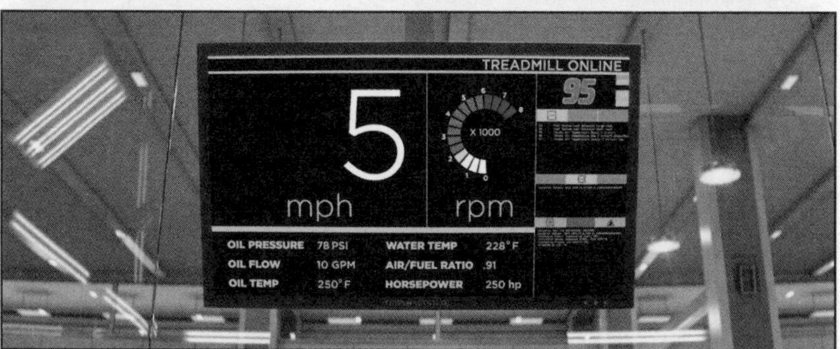
TREADMILL ONLINE
5
mph
X 1000
rpm
95
OIL PRESSURE 78 PSI
OIL FLOW 10 GPM
OIL TEMP 250° F
WATER TEMP 228° F
AIR/FUEL RATIO .91
HORSEPOWER 250 hp

TREADMILL ONLINE
95
X 1000
228° F
.91
250 hp
TREADMILL ONLINE
185
mph
rpm
012
OIL PRESSURE 79 PSI
OIL FLOW 12 GPM
OIL TEMP 260°F
WATER TEMP 240°F
AIR/FUEL RATIO .97
HORSEPOWER 607 hp

'SUP.

OKAY, DAY THREE--
TREADMILL. I'VE SET A MAXIMUM SPEED TO CONSERVE YOUR ENERGY. WHAT I WANT YOU TO DO IS VISUALIZE BEATING--

--THIS GUY.

STORM?

UH-HUH. THAT'S RIGHT! GET HIM! GET HIM, MR. MCQUEEN.

GET HIM? THIS THING'S ONLY GOING LIKE FIVE MILES AN HOUR!
5
mph rpm

WE'LL WORK UP TO THE HIGHER SPEEDS RIGHT AFTER YOU TAKE YOUR NAP.
NAP? I *DON'T* NEED A NAP!

HA! NAP.
HIT HIM WITH THE BUGS! HEH-HEH-HEH.
I AM *NOT* TAKING A NAP!!!
186
186
4

YAWN

HOW WAS YOUR NAP, MR. MCQUEEN?

IT WAS KINDA... REFRESHING, ACTUALLY.

OKAY. WHAT ARE YOU...? HEY!

YOU'VE BEEN DRIVING ON TIRES A LONG TIME. HAVE YOU EVER STOPPED TO GET TO KNOW THEM?

I'M SORRY, WHAT?

TIRES ARE INDIVIDUALS. YOU SHOULD GIVE EACH A NAME.
NAME THEM? I WON'T BE DOING THAT.

MINE ARE NAMED MARIA, JUANITA, RONALDO, AND DEBBIE RICHARDSON.

WHAT?
LONG STORY.

MAY I HAVE MY TIRES BACK SO I CAN GO ON THE SIMULATOR, PLEASE?
LIGHTYEAR
LIGHTYEAR

NAME THEM!

OKAY. UH...
...LEFTY, RIGHTY, BACKY, BACKY JR., OKAY?
DOES THIS MAKE YOU MAD?

YES, IT DOES!
USE THAT!

"AND MERGE AND YIELD, AND MERGE AND YIELD."

BEEP BEEP BEEP BEEP

...NOW YOU GOT SOME TIRE DAMAGE...

SPEED BUMP. SPEED BUMP. NOW CLEAN UP YOUR MESSY GARAGE...
...BUG IN THE WINDSHIELD. BUG IN THE WINDSHIELD.
THANK YOU, CRUZ. I'M DONE.

MERGE AND YIELD. MERGE AND YIELD...
...MR. MCQUEEN! WHERE'RE YOU GOING?
TO THE FUTURE!

OKAY! HERE WE GO. HERE WE GO! HOW DO I DO THIS? COME ON, BABY!

MR. MCQUEEN.
CRUZ, THANK YOU FOR THE OLD-MAN TRAINING--AS CRAZY AS IT WAS--BUT I'M WARMED UP ENOUGH, AND NOW I NEED YOU TO LAUNCH THIS THING.

MR. MCQUEEN, WAIT UNTIL YOU CAN HANDLE IT. PLEASE? THERE ARE NO SHORTCUTS.

OKAY. WE'LL JUST SEE ABOUT THAT--
ALL RIGHT! MY STAR RACER IS ON THE SIMULATOR!

WHY, YES I AM!
WELL, LET'S SEE YOU TAKE IT OUT FOR A SPIN.

RIGHT AWAY, MR. STERLING...

...OWNER OF THE COMPANY.

SIGH. OKAY.

HAVE FUN...

THIS IS WHAT I'M TALKIN' ABOUT--

PREPARE TO RACE.
WHOA! DIDN'T KNOW ABOUT THOSE!

THE GREEN FLAG IS OUT.
WHAT DID IT SAY? IS IT TALKING?
I DON'T SEE THE FLAG.

GO!
GO!
W-WHAT DO I DO?
GO?

OKAY. WHOA! HUH, THAT'S SENSITIVE. AH, AH...

...AH!
YOU HAVE HIT A WALL.

LAP 1 27:11
183
AIR/FUEL
HP
TORQUE
WAT. TEMP

SH-SHOULDN'T BE THIS HARD! SHOULD IT? AH!

LAP 1 05:20
YOU HAVE HIT A WALL.

YOU'RE FIGHTING THE SIMULATOR--JUST RACE LIKE YOU ALWAYS DO!

185
MPH
YOU HAVE HIT A WALL.

THERE CAN'T BE THIS MANY WALLS ON A REGULAR TRACK!

LAP 1 17:20
PASSED
YOU HAVE BEEN PASSED BY JACKSON STORM.

WAIT, STORM'S IN HERE?!

FOR MOTIVATION! STORM RACES AT 207. PICK IT UP, MR. MCQUEEN!
I'M TRYING!

SPEED
183
MPH
LAP 1
OIL TEMP
OIL PRES
OIL FLOW
ARRRR... GOOOO!
AIR/FUEL
HP
TORQUE
WAT. TEMP

...ARRRR
RUSTEZE

AH!
YOU HAVE HIT A WALL.

MR. MCQUEEN, COME DOWN FROM THERE AND WE'LL WORK YOU UP TO THIS.

SPEED
LAP 1 41:11
X1000
MPH
AH!
YOU HAVE JUMPED A BARRIER.

LAP 1 42:10
SORRY!

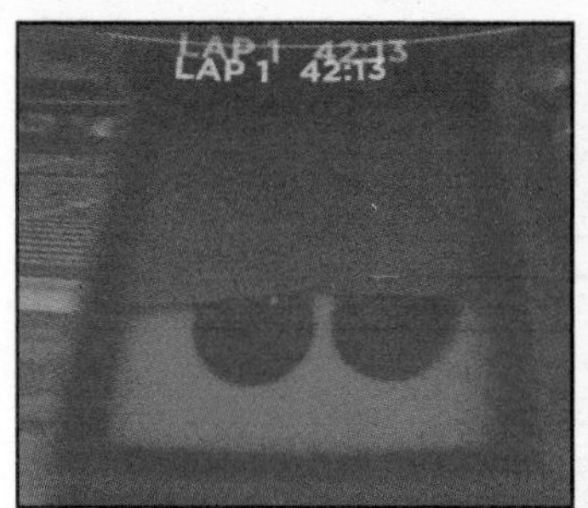
LAP 1 42:13

SPEED
RROR
MPH
LAP 1 43:00

SPEED
RROR
MPH
LAP 1 45:05
ERROR
AH!!!
YOU HAVE MAIMED TWO VEHICLES.

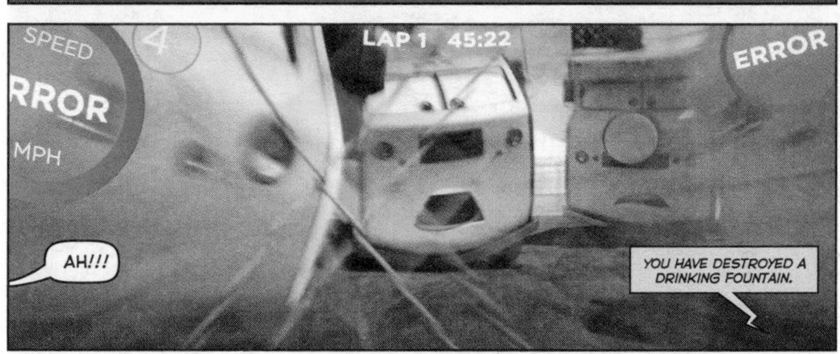
SPEED
RROR
MPH
LAP 1 45:22
ERROR
AH!!!
YOU HAVE DESTROYED A DRINKING FOUNTAIN.

AAAAAAAAAAAAAHHHHHHHHHHHHH!!!
AH! AH! AH! AH!

RROR
MPH
YOU HAVE DISABLED AN AMBULANCE.

RROR
MPH
AHHHHH!!!
YOU ARE ON FIRE.
DANGER. DANGER.

RROR
MPH
YOU ARE GOING THE WRONG WAY.
LOOK OUT!!!

SPEED
ERROR
MPH
ERROR
LAP 1 53:10
ERROR
OIL TEMP
OIL PRES
OIL FLOW
AIR/FUEL
TORQUE
TURN BACK. TURN BACK.

RROR
MPH
ERROR

SPEED
ERROR
MPH
ERROR
ERROR
ERROR
TURN IT OFF! TURN IT OFF! GET THESE THINGS OFFA ME!!!
AIR/FUEL

SPEED
ERROR
LAP 1 50:00
ERROR
CULATING
MPH

PEED
ERROR
ROR
PH
LAP 1 51:08
ERRO
WHOOOOOOA!

SPEED
ERROR
MPH

AAAAAH!

CRASH
YOU HAVE CRASHED.
YOU HAVE CRASHED.

YOU HAVE CRASHED.
ARE YOU ALL RIGHT?
I HAVE CRASHED.

BZZZZWHOOOM...

IT'S NOT EASY FOR HIM. ARE YOU SURE? GIVE HIM ANOTHER CHANCE--I CAN STILL WORK WITH HIM. CAN'T YOU JUST...? WE STILL HAVE TIME.
CRUZ, JUST RELAX. I WILL...I WILL TALK TO HIM. I KNOW HE'S YOUR PROJECT. YES. CRUZ, LET ME HANDLE THIS MY WAY. THANK YOU.
WHOA.

YOU'RE ALL WARSHED UP, MCQUEEN!

I'M-I'M SORRY. WHAT?

SAID FLOOR'S ALL WASHED UP AND CLEAN!

OH, RIGHT.

GOOD LUCK.

HEY! LIGHTNING! C'MON IN! GOT SOMETHIN' TO SHOW YA.
YOU READY?

AH... FOR WHAT?

YOU ARE ABOUT TO BECOME THE BIGGEST BRAND IN RACING.

LIGHTNING
MCGRILL
95
Lightning McQueen's
KACHOW MIX
WOW.

WE ARE TALKING SATURATION ON ALL CONTINENTS FOR EVERY DEMOGRAPHIC. MOVIE DEALS, INFOMERCIALS, PRODUCT ENDORSEMENTS...

MUD FLAPS
KACHOW
...MUD FLAPS?

OF COURSE. WE'LL BE RICH BEYOND BELIEF-- YOU THINK YOU'RE FAMOUS NOW? HA-HA.

I THOUGHT YOU'D BE MAD ABOUT THE SIMULATOR. I MEAN, THIS IS ALL GREAT, MR. STERLING...
...I GUESS, BUT I DON'T KNOW--I'VE NEVER REALLY THOUGHT OF MYSELF AS A BRAND...
BOLT5000
CARBUCHA

OH, NOR DO I. I'M A FAN. MAYBE YOUR MOST AVID. I THINK OF THIS AS YOUR LEGACY.
ERACE DIRT!
ONLINE RACING SCHOOL

HEH--IT SOUNDS LIKE SOMETHING THAT HAPPENS AFTER YOU'RE ...DONE RACING.
BOLT5000
Mr. McClean

MR. STERLING,
WHAT IS THIS ABOUT?

LOOK, LIGHTNING, I'M
NOT GONNA RACE YOU.

WHAT? WHAT
DO YOU MEAN NOT
RACE ME?
I'M NOT
GOING TO
FLORIDA?

LIGHTNING...YOU HAVE
NO IDEA HOW EXCITED I WAS
TO GET YOU HERE BECAUSE I
KNEW, I **KNEW** YOU'D BE BACK. IT
WAS GONNA BE ***THE*** COMEBACK
STORY OF THE YEAR!
BUT YOUR SPEED
AND PERFORMANCE JUST
AREN'T WHERE THEY NEED
TO BE. I'M SORRY.

WE'RE TALKING ABOUT
SPEED ON THE SIMULATOR.
LISTEN TO HOW CRAZY
THAT SOUNDS!

LOOK, I'M TRYING TO HELP YOU. AS YOUR SPONSOR, YES, BUT ALSO AS YOUR FRIEND.
YOUR RACING DAYS ARE COMING TO AN END. EVERY TIME YOU LOSE, YOU DAMAGE YOURSELF.

DAMAGE THE BRAND, YOU MEAN.

OH, LIGHTNING, COME ON. YOU'VE DONE THE WORK. NOW MOVE ON TO THE NEXT PHASE AND REAP THE REWARD.
THE RACING *IS* THE REWARD. NOT THE *STUFF*. I DON'T WANT TO CASH IN, I WANT TO FEEL THE *RUSH* OF MOVING 200 MILES AN HOUR...
...INCHES FROM THE OTHER GUYS, PUSHING MYSELF FASTER THAN *I* THOUGHT *I* COULD GO! THAT'S THE REWARD, MR. STERLING.

LOOK, I CAN DO THIS. I CAN, I PROMISE! I'LL TRAIN LIKE I DID WITH DOC! I'LL GET MY TIRES DIRTY ON EVERY DIRT TRACK FROM HERE TO FLORIDA.
OH, LIGHTNING, COME ON.

I CAN START RIGHT THERE ON FIREBALL BEACH, WHERE ALL THE OLD GREATS USED TO RACE!
"GET YOUR TIRES DIRTY." *THAT'S* HOW YOU'RE GOING TO GET FASTER THAN STORM?

YES! EXACTLY! I MEAN, SACRED DIRT, RIGHT? MR. STERLING, IF YOU CARE ABOUT MY LEGACY--THE ONE THAT DOC STARTED--YOU'LL LET ME DO THIS!
I PROMISE YOU, I WILL WIN!

I DON'T KNOW. WHAT YOU'RE ASKING-- IT'S TOO RISKY.

C'MONNNN. YOU LIKE IT, I CAN TELL. IT'S GOT THAT LITTLE COMEBACK-STORY-OF-THE-YEAR FEEL TO IT, DOESN'T IT?

ONE RACE?

IF YOU DON'T WIN AT FLORIDA, YOU'LL RETIRE?

LOOK, IF I DON'T WIN, I'LL SELL ALL THE MUD FLAPS YA GOT! BUT IF I DO WIN, I DECIDE WHEN I'M DONE. DEAL?

DEAL.

THANK YOU, MR. STERLING. YOU WON'T BE SORRY.
JUST ONE THING, AND THIS IS ONLY BECAUSE I DON'T LIKE TAKING CHANCES--YOU'RE TAKING SOMEONE WITH YOU.

LATER...
YOU TALKED HIM INTO IT! WAY TO GO, MR. MCQUEEN.
YOU COULD TALK A HUFF SNOWMOBILE HUFF INTO AN AIR CONDITIONER.

YOU'RE GOING WITH ME? WITH THAT THING?

YEAH! YOU STILL NEED MY HELP. YOU'RE BRITTLE LIKE A FOSSIL!

I DON'T NEED A TRAINER OUT HERE, CRUZ.

YOU'RE OLD. WHAT IF YOU FALL ON THIS BEACH AND CAN'T GET UP?

WELL, LIFE'S A...BEACH...AND THEN YOU DRIVE.

HA-HA! OH, MCQUEEN!
AHHH-HA-HA-HA-HA!

THANK YOU.

THIS IS BEAUTIFUL. I CAN SEE WHY MR. STERLING SAID YOU'VE WANTED TO TRAIN OUT HERE.
AS SOON AS THIS THING'S BOOTED UP, WE'LL GET YOU ON THE TREADMILL AND I'LL TRACK YOUR SPEED.

WHAT?! NO! THE WHOLE IDEA IS GETTIN' MY TIRES DIRTY--REAL RACING! I'M NOT DRIVIN' ON THAT THING WHEN I'VE GOT THE SAND... AND THE WHOLE EARTH!

OH. OKAY...

LUIGI! LET'S DO THIS!!!

WELCOME, RACERS, TO FIREBALL BEACH, HISTORIC HOME FOR TODAY'S GREAT TEST OF SPEED. OUR FINISH LINE WILL BE THE ABANDONED PIER IN THE DISTANCE.

ALL RIGHT. QUICKER THAN QUICK, FASTER THAN FAST, I AM SPEED.

THAT IS GREAT SELF-MOTIVATION--DID YOU COME UP WITH THAT?

YEAH, I DID.

ON YOUR MARK!
GET SET!

GOOOOO!

RRRRRRRR

VRRROOOM
WOOO-HOOOO!

THERE YA GO! FELT GOOD!

HEY?! WHAT WAS MY SPEED?

I DON'T KNOW.
I CAN ONLY TRACK YOU ON THE TREADMILL.

NO TREADMILLS...

OH! WHAT ABOUT HAMILTON?!
HAMILTON HERE.

WHO'S HAMILTON?
MY ELECTRONIC PERSONAL ASSISTANT-- YOU KNOW, LIKE ON YOUR PHONE. YOU DO HAVE A PHONE, DON'T YOU?

RACE CARS DON'T HAVE PHONES, CRUZ.
HAMILTON, TRACK MR. MCQUEEN'S SPEED AND REPORT IT.

TRACKING.

I'LL STAY AS CLOSE AS I CAN. YOUR SUIT WILL TRANSMIT YOUR SPEEDS TO HAMILTON.
FINE. WHATEVER. LET'S DO THIS!

QUICKER THAN QUICK, FASTER THAN FAST, I AM SPEED. COME ON, LUIGI!
LIGHTYEAR
LIGHTYEAR

ON YOUR MARK! GET SET! AND GO!

FORTY-SIX MILES PER HOUR...
SIXTY-THREE MILES PER HOUR...

OUT OF RANGE. OUT OF RANGE.

SKREEE!

HUH. THAT'S ODD...

...I DIDN'T GO!

ON SAND YOU GOTTA EASE INTO YOUR START SO YOUR TIRES CAN GRAB. OKAY?
OKAY.

YOU *DO* WORK WITH RACE CARS, DON'T YOU?
YEAH, BUT NEVER OUTSIDE.

ALL RIGHT. LET'S GO AGAIN!

GO!

FIFTY-FOUR MILES PER HOUR...
SEVENTY-FIVE MILES PER HOUR...

HUH?
OUT OF RANGE. OUT OF RANGE. OUT OF RANGE.

FSSHHH!

SORRY! GOT STUCK!

GO!

SORRY!

GO!

WHOAA-OOAA-OOA...

...WHOAA-OOAA-OOA...
SPLIIISH

...WHOAA-OOAA-OOA...
SPLOOOOOSHHH

GO!

THE BEACH
ATE ME.

ALL RIGHT, CRUZ, PICK A LINE ON THE COMPACTED SAND.
YOU GOTTA HAVE TRACTION, OR YOU'RE GONNA SPIN OUT. LET'S DO THIS THING!

ON YOUR MARK.

GET SET.

GO.

ONE TWENTY-TWO...
ONE THIRTY-FOUR...

OUT OF RANGE.

NOW WHAT?!
I DIDN'T WANT TO HIT A CRAB.

YOU GOTTA BE KIDDING ME!
WHAT? IT WAS CUTE.

AIIIIGH!!!

ALL RIGHT. ONE LAST CHANCE TO TRY THIS BEFORE IT GETS DARK.
NOW, YOU'RE GONNA TAKE OFF SLOW TO LET YOUR TIRES GRAB...
YES.

...AND PICK A STRAIGHT LINE ON HARD SAND SO YOU DON'T SPIN OUT.
UH-HUH.

AND *ALL* OF THE CRABBIES HAVE GONE NITE NITE.

MR. MCQUEEN...

ALL RIGHT.
LET'S GO AGAIN.

AND GO!
445-10.8

150 MILES PER HOUR...
...175...

...196...

...197...

WOOOOO-HOO!

ALL RIGHT, FINALLY! YOU MADE IT. CONGRATULATIONS! HOW'D I DO?
YOU TOPPED OUT AT 198.

198...THAT'S IT?!

STILL SLOWER THAN STORM.

WASTED MY WHOLE DAY...

I WOULDN'T SAY THAT. IT DID FEEL GREAT TO BE OUT HERE DOING REAL RACING!

THAT ISN'T REAL RACING! WE'RE ON A BEACH. ALL YOU DO IS GO STRAIGHT. HOW'M I GONNA GET FASTER IF I DON'T--

THUNDER HOLLOW...
THUNDER HOLLOW
GUDGEON PINES
CRAB SANCTUARY

THUNDER HOLLOW! THERE'S A DIRT TRACK THERE. THAT'S WHAT I NEED--TO RACE AGAINST ACTUAL RACERS.

NO! TOO PUBLIC! IF THE PRESS FIND YOU, THEY WILL BE LIKE MANY, MANY BUGS ON YOU!

PAPARAZZI! PTUI!

GUYS, I REALLY NEED THIS.

EH, JUST LEAVE IT TO ME, BOSS.
I AM A MASTER OF DISGUISE.

THUNDER
HOLLOW

ALL RIGHT. NEXT!
GOT MY TIRES DIRTY AT THUNDER HOLLOW
CLAK

HWEEWHEET!

BLECCH. COUGH COUGH PTOO
SPLURRP!

YOU, SIR, ARE OFFICIALLY INCOGNITO. NOBODY'S BOTHERING YOU.

OH, I CAN FEEL IT, GUYS--TONIGHT IS THE NIGHT I FIND MY SPEED!
NO MORE STRAIGHT LINES, JUST A GOOD, OLD-FASHIONED OVAL.

THE GREAT LIGHTNING MCQUEEN...

RACERS, GIT ON OVER TO THE STARTIN' LINE! PUHHHRONTO!

HEY, NOW! YOU THAT OUT-OF-TOWNER?

UH, YES! THAT'S ME. CHESTER WHIPPLEFILTER.
AND I'M...FRANCES BELTLINE.

CRUZ?! WHAT ARE YOU DOING?
I'M YOUR TRAINER. GONNA TRACK YOUR SPEED FROM THE INFIELD, WHIPPLEFILTER.

FINE, JUST STAY OUT OF THE WAY.

EXCUSE ME, SIR, WHERE ARE THE OTHER RACERS?

THEY'LL BE ALONG. WE ALWAYS LET OUR GUESTS START RIGHT UP FRONT.

WELCOME, Y'ALL CRAZY EIGHT FANS, TO THUNDER HOLLOW SPEEDWAY FOR TONIGHT'S EDITION OF...

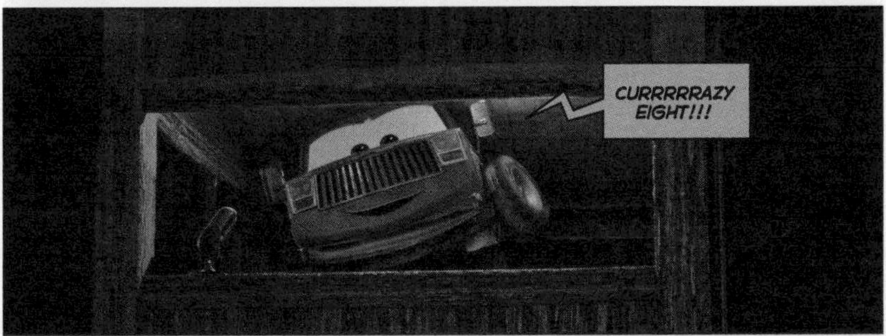
CURRRRRAZY EIGHT!!!

FWOOSH!

FOOSH!
FOOSH!

FWOOM!

DID HE SAY "CRAZY EIGHT?"

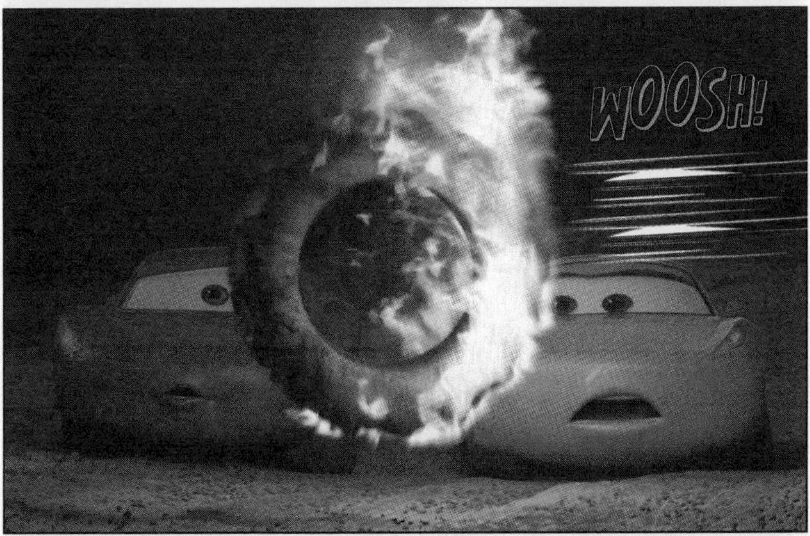
WOOSH!

RACE FANS! YOU KNOW WHAT TIME IT IS! IT'S TIME TO...MEET TONIGHT'S CHALLENGERS.

WEEE-OOO! WEEE-OOO!

HAVE A NICE TRIP!

HA-HA-HA. PROTECT AND SWERVE!

HA-HA-HAH!

WOOO-
HOOO-
HOOO!

CRUZ, THIS ISN'T WHAT I THOUGHT IT WAS --COME ON, FOLLOW ME AND WE'LL SLIP OUT.

RULE NUMBER ONE. THE GATE CLOSES? YOU RACE.

GASP

WAIT! NO, NO, NO! I'M NOT A RACER!
20
SSSSSS

RULE NUMBER TWO, LAST CAR STANDING WINS. AND RULE NUMBER THREE, NO CURSING-- IT'S FAMILY NIGHT!

EXCUSE ME, SIR...
WAIT! NO! I'M JUST A TRAINER!

AND MAKE WAY FOR THE UNDEFEATED CRAZY EIGHT CHAMPION, THE DIVA OF DEMOLITION, MISS FRITTER!!!

BOO.
AHH!

HA-HA-HA! LOOKIE HERE, BOYS! WE GOT US A COUPLE OF ROOKIES.
I'M GONNA CALL YOU MUDDY BRITCHES AND YOU LEMONADE.

HEY! NEITHER ONE OF THEM HAS A SINGLE DENT!
OH, I'M GONNA FIX THAT! HA-HA-HA!

ALL RIGHT, EVERYBODYYYY! LET'S...
...GO RAAACIN'!

AHH! AH!

HA-HA-HAA!

WHOA!

I'M ABOUT TO COMMIT A MOVING VIOLATION!

AAAAAH!

CRUZ...?

CRUZ, WHAT ARE YOU DOING?! GOTTA KEEP *MOVING!!!*

I SHOULDN'T BE OUT HERE!
MOVE, CRUZ! *MOVE!*

AAAH!

FWOOM

WHADDO I DO?! I CAN'T STEER!

TURN RIGHT TO GO LEFT! TURN RIGHT TO GO LEFT!
NO BARS
BAIL BONDS
ANY TIME • ANY CRIME

THAT DOESN'T MAKE ANY SENSE!

TURN RIGHT TO GO LEFT!!!
NO BARS
BAIL BONDS

UH...

AH!

HEY, PATTY.
OH, HEY, BILL.

AAAHHHH!
THUNDER HOLLOW

AH! AHHA!!!

NICE DAY FOR A DRIVE, HUH?!
HEY, BUDDY! GET OUTTA MY WAY!

HEY! I'M DRIVIN' HERE--
HA-HA!

YAHOOOOO!

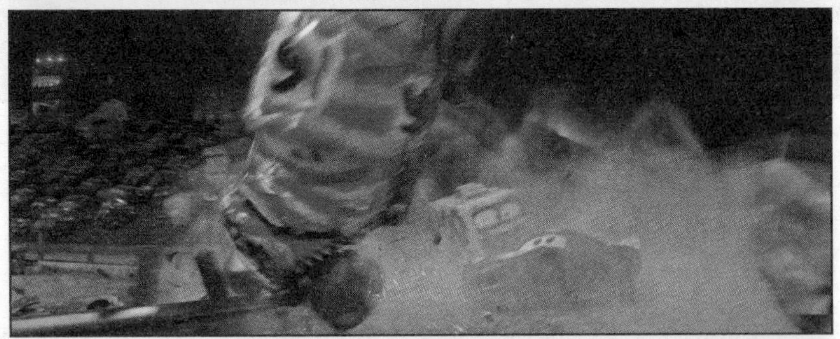

WOO-HOO!!!

LOOK AT
MY NEW HAT!

AH! AHHHHHHHHH! AHHH!

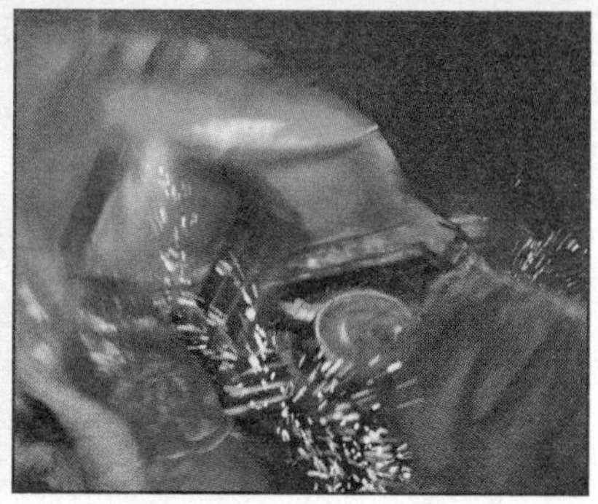

AHH-HA-HA! I'M FLYINNNNNN!!!

NO! I'M NOT FLYIN'!

I GOT IT!!!
WHOOO!

AHHHHHH!
CRUZ!

TURN RIGHT TO GO LEFT. TURN RIGHT TO GO LEFT--
20

WHOA, WHOA, WHOA, WHOA, WHOA!
TUG-N-LUG
20

AH!

OH NO.

RRRVVVV!

BUCKLE UP, EVERYBODY!

HOLLOW
Speedway
IT'S FRITTER TIME!!!

IT'S FRITTER TIME
FRITTER!
FRITTER!
FRITTER!

FRITTER TIME

WE LOVE YOU,
MISS FRITTER!

OOOOOOH
YEAH!

YOUR LICENSE PLATE'S
GONNA LOOK *REAL NICE*
IN MY COLLECTION.

OH, BOY!

OH NO...

REMEMBER, OBEY ALL APPROPRIATE STREET SIGNS!

CRUZ!

HEH-HEH...

ERRRG...

AH!

THUD!

OH, MY GRACIOUS! MISS FRITTER'S DOWN.

OHHHH!

NOBODY TOUCHES HIM! HE IS MINE!

YOU GONNA GET IT NOW, WHIPPLEFILTER!

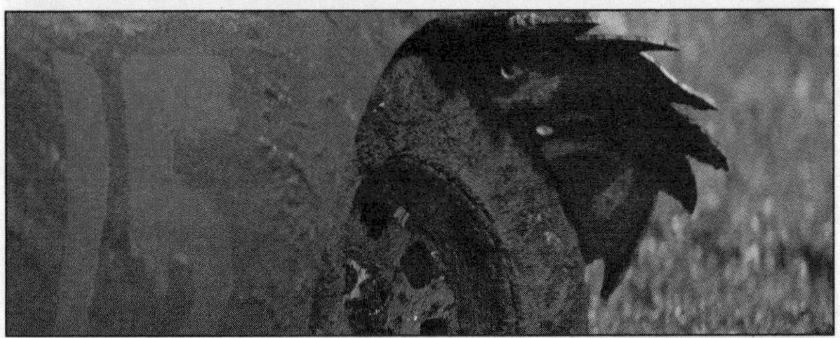

FRITTER! FRITTER! FRITTER!

COME ON, YOU CAN DO IT! COME ON, LIGHTNING, KEEP GOING. COME ON, MCQUEEN.

MISS FRITTER IS LOOKIN' TO GET UPRIGHT, FOLKS, AND SHE IS NOT PLEASED.

ERG...

THUD!
UGHHHH!!!

YOU ABOUT TO FEEL THE WRATH OF THE LOWER BELLEVILLE COUNTY UNIFIED SCHOOL DISTRICT!

HHHHRRRR!

HA-HA-HA-HA!

SPLUD!

WHUP...

NO, NO, NO! NO!

AHHHHH!!!!!!
FRITTER TIME

NO BARS
BAIL BONDS
BERRY
KRUNCH!

NO BARS
BAIL BONDS
ANY TIME • ANY CRIME
BERRY
THUD!

NO BARS
BAIL BONDS
ANY TIME • ANY CRIME
FOOMP!

LADIES AND GENTLEMEN, WE HAVE A WINNER...

...FRANCES BELTLINE!

IS THAT ME? THAT'S ME? I WON?

I WON!
ANY CRIME

CRUZ, CRUZ! NO! NO, NO, NO...

AH! WATCH OUT!

WHOA, WHOA, WHOA!!!

FSSH!

FWWWAASSSH!

FFFFSSSSHH!
WATER

FPPPPLSSH!

GURGLE...
FLLLSHHHHHH...

HUH...

HUH.

GASP!
WHIPPLEFILTER?

IT'S LIGHTNING MCQUEEN!!!

GASP!

GOT MY TIRES DIRTY
AT
THUNDER
HOLLOW

GOT MY TIRES DIRTY
AT
THUNDER

GOT MY TIRES DIRTY
AT
THUNDER
GASP!

AFTER THE DEMOLITION DERBY, MCQUEEN AND CRUZ ARE BACK ON THE ROAD.
...HOOOONK!

FANS HERE AT THUNDER HOLLOW... STILL BUZZING OVER TONIGHT'S UNEXPECTED APPEARANCE OF LIGHTNING MCQUEEN!

HE'S ALWAYS BEEN MY FAVORITE! MY GARAGE IS COVERED FROM HEAD TO TOE WITH "#95" POSTERS.

TELL OUR LISTENERS AT HOME YOU WEREN'T REALLY TRYING TO WRECK HIM, WERE YOU?
WOW. WELL, THAT WAS ONE MEMORABLE NIGHT OF RACING IN THUNDER HOLLOW, FOLKS.

WINNER
SO...TROPHY'S KINDA NICE...DON'T YA THINK?

WINNER
I MEAN, I KNOW YOU'VE GOT, LIKE, A BILLION OF THEM, SO YOU WOULD KNOW...
...I STILL CAN'T BELIEVE *I WON.*

WINNER
IT'S PRETTY SHINY. I HAVE NEVER SEEN ONE UP CLOSE. LOOKS LIKE THEY SPENT A LOT OF MONEY ON IT. I MEAN, I THINK IT'S REAL METAL!

STOP. JUST, STOP, OKAY, CRUZ? YOU DON'T EVEN KNOW...YOU DON'T HAVE ONE CLUE...

HEY! I WAS JUST TRYING TO...
WINNER

DO YOU KNOW WHAT HAPPENS IF I LOSE THIS RACE?

EVERY ***MILE*** OF THIS TRIP WAS TO GET ME FASTER THAN JACKSON STORM! FASTER!

I STARTED OFF GETTING NOWHERE FOR A *WEEK* ON A SIMULATOR! I LOSE A WHOLE DAY WITH YOU ON FIREBALL BEACH!
AND THEN, I WASTE TONIGHT IN THE CROSSHAIRS OF MISS FRITTER!

I'M STUCK IN THE SAME SPEED I WAS A MONTH AGO! I CAN'T GET ANY FASTER ***BECAUSE I'M TOO BUSY TAKING CARE OF MY TRAINER!***

THIS IS MY LAST CHANCE, CRUZ! LAST! FINAL! *FINITO!*

IF I LOSE, I NEVER GET TO DO THIS AGAIN! IF YOU WERE A RACER, YOU'D KNOW WHAT I'M TALKING ABOUT!
BUT YOU'RE NOT! SO YOU DON'T!

SLAM!

CRAAACKK!

...
MACK! PULL OVER!

HUH? NOW?

NOW!

AHHH! OKAY, OKAY! PULLING OVER! PULLING OVER!

ASK ME IF I DREAMED OF BEING A TRAINER, MR. MCQUEEN! GO AHEAD!
ASK ME IF I GOT UP IN THE DARK TO RUN LAPS BEFORE SCHOOL EVERY DAY. ASK ME IF I SAVED EVERY PENNY TO BUY A TICKET TO THE RACES WHEN THEY CAME TO TOWN.
ASK ME IF I DID THAT SO I COULD BE A TRAINER SOMEDAY!

ASK ME!

DID Y--

NO! I'VE WANTED TO BECOME A RACER FOREVER! BECAUSE OF YOU!

I USED TO WATCH YOU ON TV, FLYING THROUGH THE AIR--YOU SEEMED SO... FEARLESS...

"DREAM SMALL, CRUZ," THAT'S WHAT MY FAMILY USED TO SAY. "DREAM SMALL OR NOT AT ALL."
THEY WERE JUST TRYING TO PROTECT ME...BUT I WAS THE FASTEST KID IN TOWN, AND I WAS GONNA PROVE THEM WRONG!

WHAT HAPPENED?
WHEN I GOT TO MY FIRST RACE, I FIGURED IT OUT.

WHAT?

THAT I DIDN'T BELONG. THE OTHER RACERS LOOKED NOTHING LIKE ME--THEY WERE BIGGER AND STRONGER AND SO... CONFIDENT.
AND WHEN THEY STARTED THEIR ENGINES, THAT WAS IT...I KNEW I'D NEVER BE A RACER.
I JUST LEFT...IT WAS MY ONE SHOT, AND I DIDN'T TAKE IT.
20

YEAH, SO...I'M GONNA HEAD BACK TO THE TRAINING CENTER. I THINK WE BOTH KNOW IT'S FOR THE BEST...

...BUT CAN I ASK YOU SOMETHING?

WHAT WAS IT LIKE FOR YOU? WHEN YOU SHOWED UP TO YOUR FIRST RACE--HOW DID YOU KNOW YOU COULD DO IT?

I DON'T KNOW. I JUST... NEVER THOUGHT I COULDN'T.

I WISH I KNEW WHAT THAT FELT LIKE.

GOOD LUCK, MR. MCQUEEN.

CRUZ... CRUZ, WAIT--

"CHAMPION FOR THE AGES" CHICK HICKS HERE, COMING TO YOU LIVE FROM CHICK HICKS STUDIOS, WHERE I'M JOINED ONCE AGAIN BY NEXT-GEN RACING EXPERT, NATALIE CERTAIN.

THANKS, CHICK. PISTON CUP CHAMPION JACKSON STORM SET A NEW RECORD TODAY WHEN HE PULLED OFF THE FASTEST LAP EVER RECORDED--AN UNPRECEDENTED 213 MILES AN HOUR.
FLORIDA 500
RSN
WOW! SO, WHATTAYA THINK, CERTAIN? STORMY BOY GONNA START THE SEASON WITH ANOTHER WIN?

HIGHLY LIKELY, CHICK. BASED ON HIS RECENT RUN TIMES AND FORECASTED TRACK TEMPERATURES ON RACE DAY, STORM'S CHANCES OF WINNING ARE...

...95.2 PERCENT.
DING!
95.2 %

95.2 %
THAT LOW, HUH?!

95.2 %
OH, AND IN CASE YOU MISSED IT--

--THE TALK OF THE TRACK TONIGHT IS LIGHTNING MCQUEEN FINDING YET ANOTHER WAY TO EMBARRASS HIMSELF...AT A DEMOLITION DERBY!

WHOA. ALMOST MAKES ME FEEL SORRY FOR THE GUY--NOT REALLY! HERE'S WHAT HIS NEW SPONSOR HAD TO SAY...

EVERYONE RELAX! THE "#95"'S GONNA RACE. LIGHTNING'S JUST TAKING A SOMEWHAT... UNCONVENTIONAL...APPROACH TO THIS RACE, IS ALL. IT'S ONE OF THE THINGS HIS FANS LOVE ABOUT HIM.
RSN
RACING SPORTS NETWORK
GOT MY TIRES DIRTY AT THUNDER HOLLOW!
YEAH, RIGHT! TALK ABOUT HUMILIATING! IF I WERE OLD KA-CHOW, I WOULDN'T EVEN BOTHER TO SHOW UP IN FLORIDA.
RSN
86

THAT COULD BE FOR THE BEST, CHICK. EVEN IF HE DOES RACE, MCQUEEN'S PROBABILITY OF WINNING IS...
DING!
1.2 %
NUMBERS NEVER LIE.
...1.2 PERCENT.
WOW!
RSN

I'M WILLING TO PREDICT TONIGHT THAT LIGHTNING MCQUEEN'S RACING CAREER WILL BE OVER WITHIN THE WEEK. IT MIGHT EVEN BE OVER NOW.
I MEAN, I KNEW HIS CAREER WAS STUCK IN THE MUD...

TOW
MATER

♫♪
FIRST YOU FIND A CAN, FROM A RUSTY VAN, BUMP-BUMP, QUICKER THAN A DART, MAKE IT INTO ART, BUMP-BUMP...
...THAT'S THE WAY IT'S DONE, IT'S A LOT OF FUN, BUMP-BUMP, LIFTIN' MY FUNK, MAKIN' SCULPTURE OUTTA JUNK.

DING! DING! DING!
HUH?

WHAT'S THAT? THERE WE GO! SOMEBODY'S INTERRUPTING GENIUS!

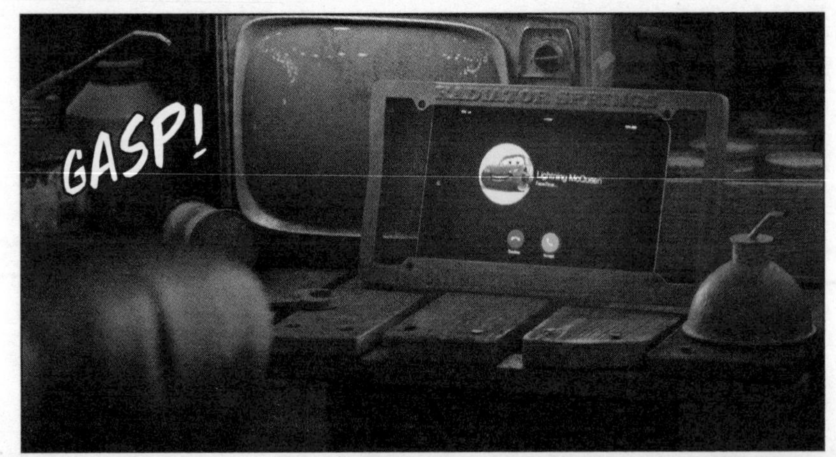
GASP!

WELL, HEY THERE, BUDDY!

HEH! MATER!

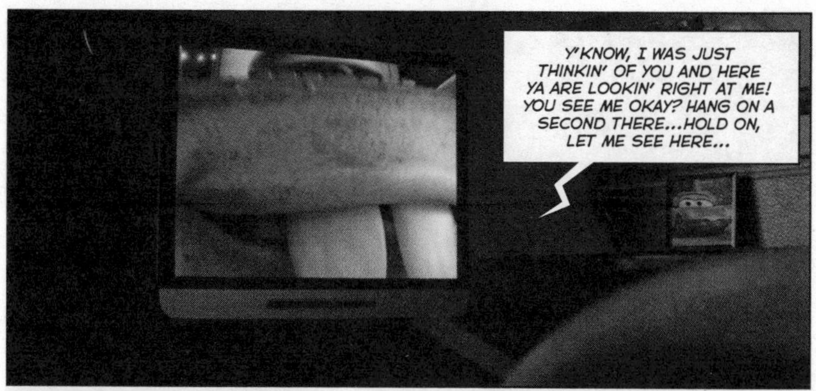
Y'KNOW, I WAS JUST THINKIN' OF YOU AND HERE YA ARE LOOKIN' RIGHT AT ME! YOU SEE ME OKAY? HANG ON A SECOND THERE...HOLD ON, LET ME SEE HERE...

...THAT BETTER?
LOOKIN' YOU STRAIGHT IN THE EYE THERE, PAL. HEY, SORRY ABOUT CALLING SO LATE...

SHOOT, NOT FOR ME, IT'S NOT! I'M ALWAYS BURNIN' THE MIDNIGHT OIL.

SO GET ME CAUGHT UP ON EVERYTHING!
WELL...ACTUALLY KINDA HOPIN' I MIGHT HEAR WHAT'S GOIN' ON BACK HOME.

WELL, NOT MUCH...NOT IF YOU DON'T COUNT SARGE AND FILLMORE TRYIN' TO RUN THE TIRE SHOP. BUT TELL LUIGI NOT TO WORRY, SARGE IS GONNA TRACK DOWN EVERY LAST TIRE THAT FILLMORE DONE GIVED AWAY.

OTHER THAN THAT, EVERYTHING'S GOOD.

HOW'S SALLY?

OH, SHE'S FINE. KEEPING BUSY AT THE CONE--SHE MISSES YA. WELL, SHOOT! WE ALL DO, WHEN YOU'RE ON THE ROAD.

YEAH. YOU KNOW, I-I'VE BEEN KINDA THINKIN' ABOUT THAT. YOU KNOW...WHAT-WHAT WE SHOULD DO WHEN I'M NOT ON THE ROAD ANYMORE?

WHAT DO YOU MEAN "NOT ON THE ROAD?"
WELL, YOU KNOW, MATER, I CAN'T DO THIS FOREVER.
HUH?!

SIGH

I'M JUST NOT GETTING ANYWHERE WITH THE TRAINING. IF ANYTHING, I'VE GOTTEN SLOWER, NOT FASTER.

AH, SHOOOT, BUDDY, IT'LL WORK OUT. JUST TELL ME WHAT THE PROBLEM IS. I'LL STAY RIGHT HERE WITH YA 'TIL WE FIX IT.

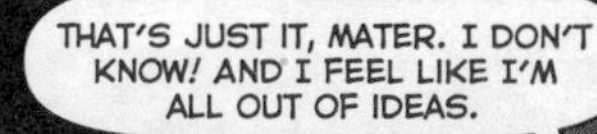
THAT'S JUST IT, MATER. I DON'T KNOW! AND I FEEL LIKE I'M ALL OUT OF IDEAS.

HMMMM, ALL RIGHT, LEMME THINK...OH! YOU KNOW WHAT I'D DO?

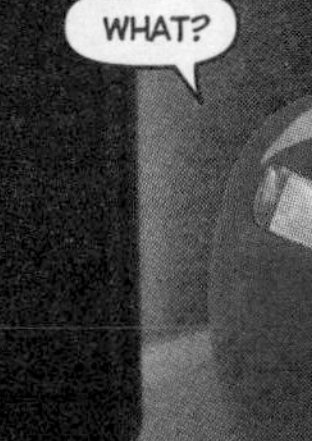
WHAT?

I DON'T KNOW. I GOT NUTHIN'.
I GUESS I AIN'T DOC WHEN IT COMES TO THAT.

I WOULD GIVE ANYTHING TO TALK TO HIM RIGHT NOW.

YEP, THERE WAS NOBODY SMARTER THAN OLD DOC. WELL, EXCEPT FOR MAYBE WHOEVER TAUGHT HIM.
YEAH... WAIT. WHAT?

I MEAN, EVERYBODY WAS TAUGHT BY SOMEBODY, RIGHT?

TAKE MY COUSIN DOYLE. HE TAUGHT ME HOW TO SING AND WHISTLE AT THE SAME TIME--HE WAS VERY MUSICAL THAT WAY.
SMOKEY...

MATER, YOU'RE BRILLIANT!

AH, WELL, IT'S ALL ABOUT THE SHAPE OF YER TEETH...
I GOTTA GO TO THOMASVILLE!

OH. WELL, GOOD. YOU KNOW ME, BUDDY, I'M ALWAYS HAPPY TO HELP. THINK I AM BETTER AT THAT THAN MOST FOLKS. YOU KNOW, TALKIN' AND STUFF.

...

...HUNH?

RUSTEZE

HEY, CRUZ.

YOU WON'T TALK ME OUT OF THIS, MR. MCQUEEN. I'M GOING BACK. I RESIGN AS YOUR TRAINER.
ALL RIGHT. I ACCEPT YOUR RESIGNATION. BYE.
20

UH, OKAY...

BUT SINCE YOU CLEARED YOUR CALENDAR, WHY DON'T YOU COME WITH US?
RUSTEZE

I'M LOOKING FOR SOMEONE NAMED SMOKEY. HOPIN' HE CAN HELP ME, MAYBE HE CAN HELP YOU, TOO.

...NAW.

COME ON... I FIXED IT...

NO. THANKS ANYWAY, BUT I'M DONE.

OKAY...BUT MAYBE *THIS* WILL CHANGE YOUR MIND!
HIT IT!

LUIGI TURNS ON THE ZUMBA MUSIC.

FIRST, I'M GONNA LOOSEN UP THESE ANCIENT JOINTS.

NO! PLEASE DON'T.

I'M SORRY, I'M SORRY, I'M SORRY THAT I YELLED--IT WASN'T YOUR FAULT THAT I ALMOST GOT KILLED...

STOP!

BUT NOW YOU'RE LEAVING AND YOU WON'T GET ON THE RAMP. YOU WON'T GET ON THE RAMP.

ALL RIGHT, I'LL GO. ALL RIGHT, I'LL GO! JUST STOP!

HOW DO YOU KNOW SMOKEY'S GONNA BE HERE?
I DON'T.

OH.
DO YOU... KNOW IF HE'S EVEN ALIVE?
NOPE.

OKAY.
SO TELL ME THIS, HOW DO YOU KNOW IF IT'S SMOKEY? IS THERE SOME...
RRC

WAIT--MACK! PULL OVER! BACK IT UP! BACK IT UP!

GOOD TO SEE YA, DOC.
THOMASVILLE
SPEEDWAY
Home of
51
Fabulous Hudson Hornet
FASTEST RACERS EVERY SUNDAY!

HEY, ISN'T THAT YOUR OLD CREW CHIEF?
HEY, CRUZ. YOU WANNA CHECK OUT THE HOME TRACK OF THE GREATEST RACER EVER?
AREN'T WE SUPPOSED TO BE LOOKING FOR SMOKEY? OH, THAT'S RIGHT, HE'S DEAD.
WE DON'T KNOW THAT.

THOMASVILLE
SPEEDWAY

KLICK
KREEK

FWAM

ARE YOU SURE YOU HAVE TIME FOR THIS?

FOR THIS...I DO.

WOOOOOW.
IF THIS TRACK
COULD TALK.

CRUZ, WHATTA
YA SAY? LET'S
TAKE A LAP.

OH-HO-
OOOOH,
YEAH!
VROOOOOM!

VROOOM

HA-HA, WHOA!

VRMMMMM

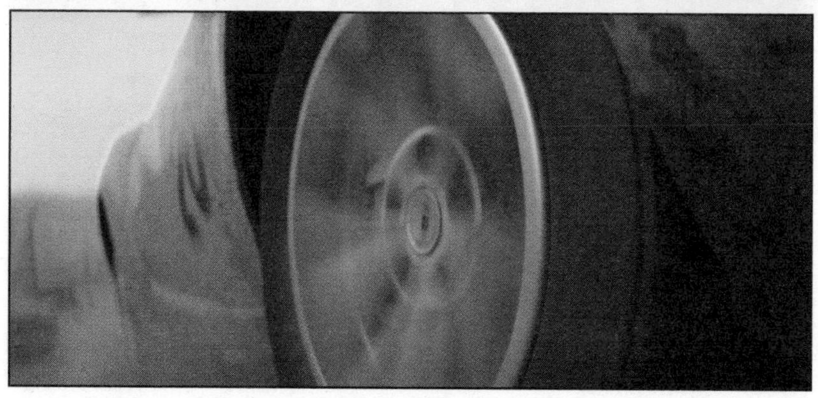

HA-HA-
HA-HA!

OOOOH! YES!
YOU NAILED IT!

WAY EASIER WITHOUT THE SCHOOL BUS OF DEATH TRYIN
TO KILL US! HA-HA-HA!
NO KIDDING!

AH...

SKKKRREEE..

..SKKKRREEE..

..SKKKDD!

UH...

STARTING TO THINK I MIGHT NEVER MEET YOU.

SMOKEY?

HE *IS* ALIVE.

I KNOW WHY YOU'RE HERE.
YOU'RE THIRSTY.

Cotter
PIN
BAR & GRILL

I TELL YOU WHAT, THESE FOLKS ARE GONNA GET A KICK OUTTA MEETIN' HUD'S BOY.
RUSTEZE

WHO'S HUD?
RUSTEZE

OH, DOC HUDSON! RIGHT.
RUSTEZE

HEY!
CREAK!

ACT CIVILIZED. WE GOT COMPANY.

WELCOME TO THOMASVILLE, SUGAR.

WOULDJA LOOK AT THAT.
WHAT?

HAD 'EM TAKE MY SHOCK ABSORBERS RIGHT OFFA ME!
I LAPPED THAT FIELD FASTER THAN A TWISTER IN A BAD MOOD...
OH, RIVER. YOU LAY IT ON THICKER EVERY TIME.
YOU TELL THAT STORY EVERY NIGHT!

THREE OF THE BIGGEST RACING LEGENDS EVER--JUNIOR "MIDNIGHT" MOON, RIVER SCOTT, LOUISE "BARNSTORMER" NASH.

LOUISE "BARNSTORMER" NASH. SHE HAD THIRTY-EIGHT WINS.

MS. NASH, IT'S A PLEASURE TO MEET YOU--

WELL, AS I LIVE AND BREATHE, IF IT AIN'T LIGHTNING MCQUEEN.

YOU'VE HAD A TOUGH YEAR, HAVEN'T YA?

OH...UH...
WELL--

SHOULDN'T YOU BE RUNNIN' PRACTICE LAPS IN FLORIDA BY NOW?

YEAH... SURE, BUT--

THEY'RE HERE TO STEAL OUR SECRETS.
LOOKIN' FOR YOUR LOST MOJO?

YOU DON'T MINCE WORDS AROUND HERE, DO YOU?

HA! TRUTH IS ALWAYS QUICKER, KID.

GUIDO! SHE'S AN ANGEL.

LOU WON'T ADMIT THIS, BUT SHE USED TO HAVE SERIOUS EYES FOR HUD!
OHHHH, REALLY?

EVEN IF I DID, IT WOULDN'TA MATTERED. HUD DIDN'T LIKE FAST WOMEN...AND THAT LEFT ME OUT!

BUT OL' LOU WASN'T JUST FAST, SHE WAS FEARLESS.

94
THE SECOND I SAW MY FIRST RACE, I JUST KNEW I HAD TO GET IN THERE. 'COURSE THE FELLAS IN CHARGE DIDN'T LIKE THE IDEA OF A LADY RACER SHOWIN' 'EM UP, SO THEY WOULDN'T LET ME HAVE A NUMBER.

WHAT DID YOU DO?

I STOLE ONE!

WHAT?!
WOW.

LIFE'S TOO SHORT TO TAKE "NO" FOR AN ANSWER.
RIGHT, RIVER?

IF WE HAD WAITED FOR AN INVITATION, WE MIGHTA NEVER RACED.

AND ONCE WE GOT ON THE TRACK, WE DIDN'T WANT TO LEAVE.

I THINK HAT'S HOW DOC FELT, TOO.

YOU SHOULDA SEEN HIM WHEN HE FIRST CAME TO TOWN, SHINY BLUE PAINT--NOT JUST THE HUDSON HORNET. HE WAS ALREADY CALLING HIMSELF...

...THE *FABULOUS* HUDSON HORNET!

NOT FOR LONG.
HOO-HOO! OH, DID WE EVER RIDE HIM ON THAT.
HUD WAS THE FASTEST RACER THIS SIDE OF THE MISSISSIPPI!

UNTIL HE WASN'T.

WHAT?

EVERYTHING CHANGED WHEN THE ROOKIE SHOWED UP.

SPEEDWAY

"TOOK HUD ALL OF NO TIME TO WORK HIS WAY THROUGH THE BEST RACERS IN BOTH CAROLINAS.
"PAST RIVER...

"...PAST LOU...
"...EVEN JUNIOR...

"...BUT THERE WAS STILL THE ROOKIE TO DEAL WITH.
"HE TRIED SLAMMING HIM INTO THE WALL.
"BUT HUD NEVER TOUCHED ANY WALL...

"...UNLESS HE
WANTED TO."
300

THAT ROOKIE NEVER
SAW ANYTHING LIKE
THAT BEFORE.

DOC DID THAT?!
WHOA! ARE YOU KIDDING?!

COULDN'T WIPE THE SMILE OFF HIS FACE FOR A WEEK AFTER THAT!

I WISH I COULD HAVE SEEN HIM LIKE THAT.

LIKE WHAT?

SO HAPPY.

LATER...

YA DIDN'T COME ALL THIS WAY FOR A QUART OF OIL, DID YA?

I NEED YOUR HELP, SMOKEY.
YEAH? WHAT KIND OF HELP?

THAT'S JUST IT, I'M NOT SURE. ALL I KNOW IS IF I LOSE IN FLORIDA, IT'S ALL OVER FOR ME. WHAT HAPPENED TO DOC WILL HAPPEN TO ME.

WHAT DID HAPPEN TO HIM?

YOU KNOW, RACING WAS THE BEST PART OF HIS LIFE, AND WHEN IT ENDED HE...WELL, WE BOTH KNOW HE WAS NEVER THE SAME AFTER THAT.

IS THAT WHAT YOU THINK?

COME ON...

...I WANNA SHOW YOU SOMETHIN'.

YOU GOT THE FIRST PART RIGHT. THE CRASH BROKE HUD'S BODY, AND THE NO-MORE-RACING BROKE HIS HEART.
HE CUT HIMSELF OFF, DISAPPEARED TO RADIATOR SPRINGS...SON OF A GUN DIDN'T TALK TO ME FOR FIFTY YEARS.

BUT THEN ONE DAY, THE LETTERS STARTED COMIN' IN. AND EVERY LAST ONE OF 'EM WAS ABOUT YOU.

YEAH. HUD LOVED RACIN', BUT COACHIN' YOU? I'D NEVER SEEN THE OLD GRUMP SO HAPPY.

RACING WASN'T THE BEST PART OF HUD'S LIFE--
DOES IT AGAIN!

--YOU WERE.

Old-School Moves Meet New-School Style
'I OWE IT ALL TO DOC'
HUDSON HOR
IS THE TALK O
Lightning shares
Lightning McQueen talks track and tactics and what

HUDSON HORNET PROTÉGÉ IS THE TALK OF THE TRACK
'I OWE IT ALL TO DOC'
Lightning McQueen talks track and tactics and what it's like working with the Fabulous Hudson H
DOES IT AGA

RUSTEZE

the top of the mo
dustry has been
revolution than a
And true to the de
revolution.
McQUEEN
UDSON

YOU READY TO BLOW OUT A LITTLE CARBON THERE, BOY?

YOU GIVE IT TOO MUCH THROTTLE, YOU IN THE TULIPS.

HEY, LIGHTNING, YOU MIGHT WANT TO TAKE NOTES ON THIS ONE.
FABULOUS HUDSON HORNET

McQUEEN
YOU GOT A LOTTA STUFF, KID.

HUD SAW SOMETHIN' IN YOU THAT YOU DON'T EVEN SEE IN YOURSELF. ARE YOU READY TO GO FIND IT?

YES, SIR.

MOMENTS LATER, MCQUEEN, CRUZ, AND SMOKEY START TO TRAIN ON THE THOMASVILLE TRACK.

ALL RIGHT, ALL RIGHT. BRING IT BACK.
LESSON ONE--
--YOU'RE OLD. ACCEPT IT.

I TOLD HIM THAT.
HEH-HEH. HE'S PROBABLY LOSING HIS HEARING.

HE SAID YOU'RE OLD, AND LOSING YOUR...
I HEARD HIM.

YOU'LL NEVER BE AS FAST AS STORM, BUT YOU CAN BE SMARTER THAN HIM.

OKAY, WHAT DO I GOTTA DO?

THEY SAID YOU WERE IN A DEMOLITION DERBY.
SMOKEY'S

YEAH, IT WAS TERRIBLE AND I ALMOST--
YA SURE? 'CAUSE THERE'S NOT A SCRATCH ON YA.
FUNNY WHAT A RACER CAN DO WHEN HE'S NOT OVERTHINKING THINGS.

MEANWHILE, IN FLORIDA.

"SHANNON SPOKES HERE AT FLORIDA INTERNATIONAL SPEEDWAY, WHERE JACKSON STORM CLOCKED 214 MILES PER HOUR TODAY."
YOU WANNA BEAT JACKSON STORM, YOU NEED SOMEONE TO STAND IN FOR HIM...
...LIKE A SPARRING PARTNER.

STORM

...

NICE JOB!
LOOKIN' GOOD!
ALL RIGHT!

RRRRRRRRR
WHOAH! YEAH!

HEH-HEH. WITH NO MUFFLER, YA EVEN SOUND LIKE STORM!
SMOKEY'S

RRRRRRRRR
YOU'RE GOIN' *DOWN,* MCQUEEN. GET THAT ARTHRITIS-RIDDLED KEISTER ONTO THAT TRACK SO I CAN PUT YOU INTO THE OLD FOLKS HOME AGAINST YOUR WILL!

HOW WAS THAT?

THAT'LL WORK.
WORKED FOR ME.

I'M GOOD.
YEP, THAT'LL DO.
DID YOU HEAR WHAT SHE SAID?

YOU DIDN'T SHOW UP IN FLORIDA FOR QUALIFYING, SO YOU'LL BE STARTIN' DEAD LAST. I'LL GIVE YOU THREE LAPS TO CATCH HER.

GO THROUGH THE ENTIRE FIELD IN THREE LAPS?

YOU WANNA BEAT STORM OR NOT?

YES! OF COURSE I DO--

HEH-HEH. WELL THEN, GO!

CRUZ TAKES
OFF, MCQUEEN
HOT ON HER TAIL.

WHOA!

ALL RIGHT...LOOKS LIKE WE GOT SOME WORK TO DO.

LOOK ALIVE! THE REFLEXES ARE THE FIRST THING TO GO!
FWSSH!

FOOMP!
AH!!! WHOA! AHHH!

WHY ARE WE IN A FIELD?

SNEAK THROUGH THAT WINDOW!

WHAT DOES THAT MEAN?
I DON'T KNOW!

GO!
RRRRRRRRR

MOOO!
MOOO!

MOOO!
AHHHH!!!
MOOO!
MOOO!
NOT COOL, MAN, NOT COOL!

MOOO!
MOOO!
MOOO!
MOOO!
MOOO!
MOOO!

MOOO!
MOOO!
MOOO!
MOOO!
MOOO!

MOOO!
MOOO!
MOOO!
MOOO!
MOOO!
MOOO!

MOOO!
MOOO!
MOOO!
MOOO!
MOOO!
MOOO!

RUN IT BACK.

ONLY TWO DAYS LEFT, KID. YOU GOTTA WORK HARDER!

MEANWHILE, BACK IN FLORIDA, JACKSON STORM CONTINUES HIS TRAINING.

210
4
70/

210
70/

WAIT, WAIT, WAIT, WHO WAS THAT?
I PUT MCQUEEN IN THERE! GIVE YA SOME REAL COMPETITION!

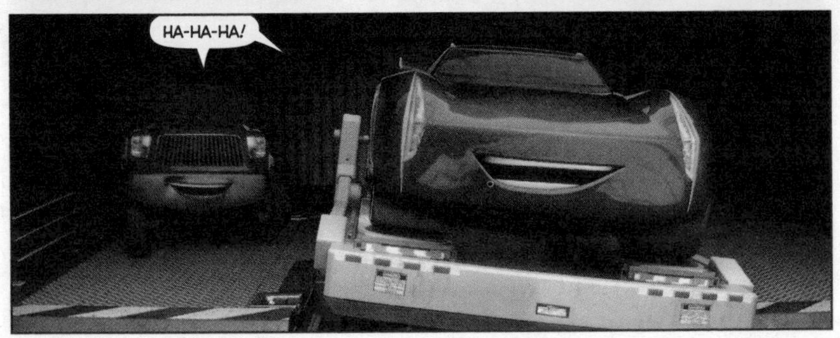
HA-HA-HA!

LIGHTYEAR

LIGHTYEAR

HUD WAS A MASTER OF LETTING THE OTHER CARS DO THE WORK FOR HIM.

HE USED TO SAY CLING TO 'EM LIKE YOU WAS TWO JUNE BUGS ON A SUMMER NIGHT.
HE STOLE THAT FROM ME!

DRAFTING? I'VE NEVER HAD TO DO THAT.

YEAH, THAT'S WHEN YOU WERE FAST--NOW YOU'RE SLOW.

AND OLD.
AND RICKETY.
AND DILAPIDATED.

OKAY, OKAY! I GET IT.

THE NEW YOU HAS TO LOOK FOR OPPORTUNITIES YOU NEVER KNEW WERE THERE.

MOOO!

"SNEAK THROUGH THE WINDOW!"

SNEAK THROUGH THE WINDOW...
WHAT?!

WHEN A WINDOW OPENS, TAKE IT!

WHOA-HO!
AIIEEE!

I MADE IT!
ALL RIGHT!

LET'S GO! LET'S MOVE!

FWSSH!

FOOMP!

FOOMP!

FWSSH!
THERE YA GO! REFLEXES

ALL RIGHT, GUIDO, TURN UP THE HEAT!

OKAYYY!

WHOAA!!!

AH!
KRUNK!

AAHH!
sPLUNGG!

ALL RIGHT! LOOK WHO FINALLY SHOWED UP!
THUNK!

THIS IS WHERE WE CUT OUR RACING TEETH.
IN THE WOODS?

LET'S JUST SAY THE MOON WAS ALWAYS SHINING ON US.
HUH?

IF THE MOON DIDN'T SHINE, WE DIDN'T HAVE TO GO IN--

--OH, NEVER MIND.
WE RAN MOONSHINE, DUMMY!

OHHHHH.

BY THE WAY,
NO LIGHTS.

INSTINCT
ONLY.

YAY!
YIPPEE!

WHOA, WHOA, WHOA,
WHOA, WHOA!
AH! HEY,
HEY, HEY! WHOA,
WHOA, WHOA!

AHHHHHH!
AH--AH--AH!

AAH! NO!

NO, NO, NO!

AAH!

AAAH! AAAAAA!

HHH!
SCREEE!

ALL RIGHT...
I-I THINK...

UH...

KRRRRSSH!
HA-
HA-HA

HAH!

HA-HA-
HA-HA-HA! WOO!
YEAH!

RIIIP...
95

RRRRRIPPP!

SWWWWOOM!

WOO-HOO-HOO-HOOO!!!

PRE-RACE COVERAGE
LIVE
SHANNON SPOKES
REPORTING FROM THE
MCQUEEN'S STILL NOT HERE? DIDN'T HE PULL THIS WHEN HE WAS A ROOKIE? AT LEAST, THAT'S WHAT MY GRANDFATHER TOLD ME.
HOME OF
RSN

PRE-RACE COVERAGE
LIVE
MAYBE IT'S BEST HE DOESN'T SHOW UP, YOU KNOW, AFTER HOW LAST SEASON ENDED.
INTERNATIONAL SUPER SPEEDWAY
RSN

PRE-RACE COVERAGE
LIVE
LEMME PUT IT THIS WAY--I'M NOT LOSING *ANY* SLEEP WONDERING WHERE LIGHTNING MCQUEEN IS.
INTERNATIONAL SUPER SPEEDWAY
VITOLINE 24
RSN

ALL RIGHT! WE GOT TIME FOR ONE LAST RACE.

HURRY THIS ALONG, BOSS, WE GOTTA GET YOU TO FLORIDA.
RUSTEZE

GO!

VRRRM

SCREEE!

VRRRM!

VRRRR!

SSSKKKDDD!

HRR...

VSSH!

WHRRRMM!
VRRREEE!

COME ON, BOY. COME ON!

VVVMMM!
SCREEEE!

WHRRRMM!
VVVRRM!

THERE YOU GO, BOY! THERE YOU GO!

VWWWSH!

VVVRRM!

VVRM!

VVRM!
WHRRRMM!

VVRM!
VVVWWWRRRMM!

"MCQUEEN IS FADING...

"...MCQUEEN IS FADING...
STORM

"...FADING FAST..."

VWWWSH!

WOOOO-HOOO!!! YES!!! DID YOU SEE THAT? THAT WAS INCREDI...

OH, UH, SORRY...

I DIDN'T MEAN TO...

HEY, UH, BOSS. IT'S TIME TO...HIT THE ROAD.
YEAH. I, UH, I WANT TO THANK EVERYONE FOR THE TRAINING.

WE BETTER GET GOING TO FLORIDA.

"WELCOME TO RACING'S GREATEST DAY! WE'RE BEACHSIDE AT THE FLORIDA INTERNATIONAL SPEEDWAY TO KICK OFF A NEW SEASON OF PISTON CUP RACING. IT'S THE FLORIDA 500."

"FORTY-THREE CARS AND A QUARTER MILLION FANS AWAIT TODAY'S INTENSE CONTEST OF STRATEGY, SKILL, BUT MOST OF ALL, SPEED...

"THIS CROWD IS IN FOR ONE GREAT DAY OF RACING!"

RSN
LIVE
"I'M BOB CUTLASS, JOINED AS ALWAYS BY MY BROADCASTING PARTNER, DARRELL CARTRIP, AND STAT SENSATION NATALIE CERTAIN."
EST OF THE TRACK, JACKSON STORM POISED TO BLOW AWAY THE COMPETITION DURING THIS YEAR'S PISTON CUP SERIES. RUMORS THUNDER AS CROWD WAITS FOR THE

JACKSON STORM
2.0
DEFENDING CHAMPION
BY THE NUMBERS
LIVE STATS
PISTON CUP WINS
1
"I'VE NEVER SEEN THE NUMBERS LINE UP FOR STORM LIKE THEY DO TODAY, BOB. STORM SHOULD BE 98.6 PERCENT UNSTOPPABLE."

"WELL, DON'T OVERLOOK LIGHTNING MCQUEEN?"

WHIPPLEFILTER! WOO-HOO!!!

"WE'VE HEARD STORIES OF THE UNUSUAL WAY MCQUEEN TRAINED TO GET HERE...

"...NOW THE QUESTION IS...

"...DID IT WORK?"

SPEED.
I. AM.
SPEED?

SIGH
KNOCK
KNOCK
KNOCK
HEY, BOSS, THEY'RE, UH, CALLING RACERS TO THE TRACK!

HEY, MCQUEEN! WIN ONE FOR US OLD GUYS!

WILL DO, JEFF.

HEY THERE, BUDDY!
VITOLINE

HEY, GUYS...

STICKERS

HEY, SAL.

YOU OKAY?

YEAH, YEAH, ABSOLUTELY.
REALLY?
LISTEN, YOU'RE GONNA DO GREAT TODAY. AND NO MATTER WHAT HAPPENS...
...I'M GONNA MOVE ONTO THE NEXT ROOKIE AND FORGET I EVER KNEW YOU.

I'M GLAD YOU'RE HERE.

OOOOH, NICE COSTUME! COME HERE, LET'S GET A PICTURE. IT'S SO GREAT TO MEET MY NUMBER-ONE FAN...

UGH. WHAT A JERK.

SHE'S NOT A FAN, STORM.

OH! HEY THERE, CHAMP! I HEAR YOU'RE SELLIN' MUD FLAPS AFTER TODAY. IS THAT TRUE?

HEY, YOU PUT ME DOWN FOR THE FIRST CASE, OKAY?

LIIIIIGHTNIIING!

LIIIIIGHTNING MCQUEEEEEEEN!!!

HEY, LIGHTNING!

HUNH?

HEY, MR.
STERLING.

TO THE FUTURE,
EH, CHAMP?
73
95

YEAH...TO
THE FUTURE.
HEY, JUST FOCUS
ON WHAT YOU'RE
HERE TO DO, KID.

THANKS,
SMOKEY.
NOW, GO, MAKE
HUD PROUD!
YOU GOT
IT.
RUSTEZE
95 RUSTEZE 95

OFFICIAL

OFFICIAL

"BOOGITY, BOOGITY, BOOGITY, LET'S GO RACIN'!"

THERE YA GO, KID.

17 5
18 121
19 95
20
21 84

117
121

95

15 34
16 5
17 95
18 117
19 121
"LIGHTNING MCQUEEN IS MAKING STEADY PROGRESS IN THE EARLY PARTS OF THIS RACE."

"WELL, IT WON'T BE ENOUGH TO CATCH STORM."

"CONSIDERING HE STARTED DEAD LAST, I DON'T THINK HE'S DOING HALF BAD OUT THERE!"

NOT TOO SHABBY! YOU KEEP THIS UP, YOU'LL FINISH IN THE TOP TEN!

TOP TEN'S NOT GONNA CUT IT, SMOKEY. I GOTTA GO ALL THE WAY!

SO DIG IN! REMEMBER YOUR TRAINING! FIND STORM AND CHASE HIM DOWN!

OH! TELL HIM HE HAS THREE LAPS TO CATCH ME!

CRUZ SAYS YOU'VE GOT THREE LAPS TO CATCH HER.

VRRRRR

VVVRRRRMMM!
TELL HER THANKS.

WOOO!
STORM

CRUZ.
WHAT ARE YOU DOING HERE?
I'D LIKE YOU TO HEAD BACK TO THE TRAINING CENTER RIGHT AWAY.
95

BUT, WHY?
95

BECAUSE I NEED YOU TO GET KURT UP TO SPEED FOR THE RACE NEXT WEEKEND--
--UM, WAIT, NOT KURT. HE'S THE BUG GUY, RIGHT? THE OTHER ONE--RONALD--YES!
I WANT TO STAY AND WATCH--
95

HEH. NOT GONNA HAPPEN, CRUZ. NOW GO...
Rev-N-Go
73

BUT MR. MCQUEEN STILL HAS A CHANCE--

JUST GO DO YOUR JOB.

AND TAKE OFF THAT SPOILER AND THOSE RACING TIRES. YOU LOOK RIDICULOUS!
YOU ARE A TRAINER, REMEMBER?

NOT A RACER.

WINNER
"IF YOU WERE A RACER,
YOU'D KNOW WHAT I'M TALKING
ABOUT! BUT YOU'RE NOT!
SO YOU DON'T!"

"OH, NO, SHE'S NOT A
RACER, SHE'S A TRAINER."
TOP SPEED
193
4
LAP 5 28:26

"I'VE WANTED TO BECOME A RACER FOREVER. BECAUSE OF YOU!"
20

STORM

SMOKEY'S
GARAGE
"WOOOO-HOOO!!!"
20

"IT WAS MY ONE SHOT
AND I DIDN'T TAKE IT."

WRECK IN TURN TWO! WRECK IN TURN TWO. GO LOW, GO LOW!

HH!

WAAAAUGH!
SSQUEEEAL!

AAH!

HHR!

WHEW!

KID, YOU OKAY?

SMOKEY, I NEED CRUZ!
NEVER MIND THAT NOW, KID--

NO! I NEED HER BACK HERE. NOW! GET HER BACK!

CAUTION
CAUTION
CAUTION

"THE YELLOW FLAG IS STILL OUT, FOLKS. WRECKED CARS EVERYWHERE. WE'RE TRYING TO FIGURE OUT WHICH RACERS ARE ABLE TO CONTINUE."

HAMILTON HERE. CALL FROM CHESTER WHIPPLEFILTER.
CHESTER WHI-- MR. MCQUEEN?!

"WELL, THE GREEN LIGHT'S ON, PIT ROAD IS OPEN, AND EVERYBODY'S COMIN' IN."
GET READY, GUYS. LUIGI, GUIDO--TIRES! FILLMORE--FUEL!

OKAY, I'M HERE. WHAT'S GOING ON?
EZE
95

NO. NOT ME...
Rust-eze
95

...HER.
OH.
DIRT TRACK TIRE

WHAT?

WHAT IS SHE DOING BACK HERE?!

COME ON, GUYS! GET HER SET UP. QUICKLY!
RUSTEZE
DIRT TRACK

OKAY! TIRES!
WAIT, WHAT'S HAPPENING?

HEY, RAMONE! YOU GOT YOUR PAINTS?

YOU KNOW I DO.

GUYS! WHAT ARE YOU DOING?
JUST THEN, ALL THE OTHER RACERS FINISH THEIR PIT STOPS AND PULL BACK ONTO THE TRACK.

"MAN, I DON'T UNDERSTAND IT! MCQUEEN'S JUST SITTIN' THERE. SOMETHING MUST BE WRONG."

MR. MCQUEEN?

TODAY'S THE DAY, CRUZ. YOU'RE GETTING YOUR SHOT.

WHAT?!

I STARTED THIS RACE, AND YOU'RE GONNA FINISH IT.

WHAT?!? SHE'LL DAMAGE THE BRAND! SHE'S JUST A TRAINER!

NO, SHE'S A RACER. JUST TOOK ME A WHILE TO SEE IT.

THAT CAN'T BE LEGAL!

HA-HAH. THE RULES ONLY SAY THE NUMBER HAS TO BE OUT THERE. DOESN'T SAY WHO HAS TO WEAR IT.

NO! YOU CAN'T DO THAT--

STER-LING
KLUNK!

AH!

DID I EVER TELL YOU HOW MUCH I LOVE YOUR MUD FLAPS?

GOT MY FISHIN' FLAPS, GOT MY CHURCH FLAPS...

...MY GOING OUT AND EATIN' FLAPS...
OUT OF MY WAY, YOU BUMPKIN!

"COME ON, GUYS! WE GOTTA GET HER OUT THERE! LET'S GO!"

TIRES, CHECK!

FUEL, CHECK!

RAMONE?

EH--BEST I COULD DO IN THE TIME FRAME, BOSS.

YEAH...

...THAT'LL WORK.

WHY ARE YOU DOING THIS? YOU SAID IT YOURSELF-- THIS MIGHT BE YOUR LAST CHANCE.

WHICH MAKES IT MY LAST CHANCE TO GIVE YOU YOUR FIRST CHANCE, CRUZ. AND THIS TIME, I WANT YOU TO TAKE IT.
LIGHTYEAR

SHE'S GOTTA BEAT THAT PACE CAR OUT!
SMOKEY'S
AUTOMOTIVE SERVICE

NO! NO!
NO! YOU CAN'T
DO THAT...

NOW OR NEVER!
SMOKEY'S
AUTOMOTIVE
SERVICE

WHAT DO
YOU SAY?

VITOLINE

ACK!
WWWRRRMMMM!

WHOA. HEY! THIRTY-FIVE MILES PER HOUR PIT SPEED!

I KNEW THAT!

"LIGHTNING MCQUEEN'S TEAM HAS ENTERED A DIFFERENT CAR SPORTING THE '#95!'"
"I DON'T BELIEVE WHAT I'M SEEING!"

CRUZ

YOU'RE WATCHING THIS, RIGHT?
2.0

WHAT, THE GIRL IN THE ***COSTUME?!*** YOU'RE KIDDING ME! HE PUT HER IN THE RACE?!

AAH!
VVRRRRRRRMMMM!

HPH! HPH! HHHHUUU!
RRRRRRRMMMM!

CRUZ, WHATTA YA DOING? COME ON, PICK IT UP!

YOU GOTTA GO FASTER!

OKAY, CALL HER FRANCES BELTLINE AND TELL HER THE SCHOOL BUS OF DEATH IS AFTER HER!

WHAT? NO!

TRUST ME.

UH, FRANCES BELTLINE, THE SCHOOL BUS OF DEATH IS AFTER YA!

WHAT? OH, UH-HUH. RIGHT.

WWWRRRRMMMM!

OKAY, THAT WAS DIFFERENT.

CRUZ, YOU'RE LOOKIN' TOO TIGHT NOW. COME ON, LOOSEN UP!

WHAT? NO.
TELL HER SHE'S A FLUFFY CLOUD.

SMOKEY, TELL HER.

UH, CRUZ, YOU ARE A FLUFFY CLOUD.

OH...RIGHT, TOO TIGHT. I'M A FLUFFY CLOUD. I'M A FLUFFY CLOUD.

AAGGH!
SKRREEE!

ANTICIPATE YOUR TURNS. CRUZ, GET YOUR HEAD IN THE RACE.
WAIT WAIT WAIT-- TELL HER SHE'S ON A BEACH AND ALL THE LITTLE CRABBIES HAVE GONE NITE NITE.

NO! I AIN'T SAYING THAT! YOU TELL HER!

ALL RIGHT, CRUZ... THE BEACH. I NEED YOU TO THINK OF THE BEACH!
HUNH?

MR. MCQUEEN!

YEAH, YEAH! IT'S ME. REMEMBER THE BEACH!
RUSTEZE

OH, UH-HUH. PICK A LINE. STICK TO IT. GOT IT!

ALL RIGHT, NOT TOO BAD...

HUFF HUFF

AGH!

THIS IS *NOTHING* LIKE THE SIMULATOR!

YOU GOT EVERY TOOL YOU NEED. NOW REMEMBER THOMASVILLE.

THOMASVILLE?

YEAH, SNEAK THROUGH THE WINDOW.

NOW *THAT* I UNDERSTAND!

SNEAK THROUGH THE WINDOW.

MMOOO!

HA-HA!

WWRRM!

VVRRRWWM!

THERE WE GO!

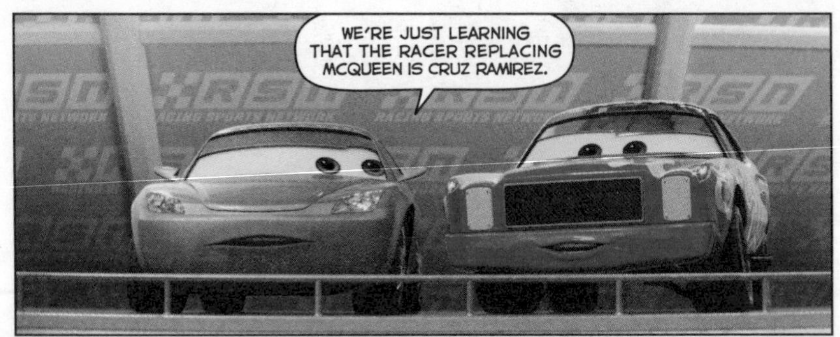
WE'RE JUST LEARNING THAT THE RACER REPLACING MCQUEEN IS CRUZ RAMIREZ.

THIS IS...

...HER VERY FIRST RACE!

"ACTUALLY, DARRELL, IT SAYS HERE SHE DOES HAVE ONE WIN UNDER HER BELT. AT A PLACE CALLED... THUNDER HOLLOW?"

WOO-HOO! THUNDER HOLLOW! SHE SAID THUNDER HOLLOW!
ONE WAY

TRY MOVIN' HALF A LANE. HALF A LANE.
GOT IT!

ALL RIGHT. WATCH THAT LAP CAR--HE'S GONNA GO HIGH.

VRRRM!

VRRRWWM!

VVVRRRWWM!

GO LOW, GO LOW!

WWVRRRM!

NICE JOB!

YOU ARE SMOKING THESE GUYS!
NOW, WATCH OUT BY THE WALL, IT'S A LITTLE SLICK THERE. WATCH IT, WATCH IT, WATCH IT!

YOU HAVE HIT A WALL. YOU HAVE HIT A WALL.

HA-HA! JUST BEING AGGRESSIVE!

12 54
13 68
14 95
15 90
16 4
17 48
18 39

OKAY, I WANT YOU TO PIT. WATCH YOUR RPMS.
GET OUT OF THE GAS! ON THE BRAKE! ON THE BRAKE!

UH, WE'RE BACK HERE.
RUSTEZE
ZOOOM!

SORRY!
ALL RIGHT, PICK 'EM OFF ONE AT A TIME.

GO! GO! GO!
VRRRR

VVRRRRMM
THAT'S IT, NICE AND STRAIGHT. WOO-HOO! GO! GO! GO! GO!

VVVWWWRRMM

SMOKEY, YOU WATCHING?
RUST-EZE

HEY! JUST WANT TO LET YOU KNOW, RAMIREZ IS MOVING UP TOWARD YOU.

WHY SHOULD I CARE?
BECAUSE NOW SHE'S IN THE TOP TEN!

WWWRRRRM!

LAP 491
1 20
2
3 00
4 95

WOOOO!

OKAY, OKAY, NOW YOU'RE COMING UP ON THE LEADERS...

RAMIREZ'S UP TO FOURTH.
FOURTH?
HUH.

GET 'ER DONE!!!

RAMIREZ'S IN THIRD.

VVVMMM!

WHAT ARE YOU DOING, STORM?

HEY! COSTUME GIRL! YOU KNOW, AT FIRST I THOUGHT YOU WERE OUT HERE 'CAUSE YOUR GPS WAS BROKEN.

DON'T LISTEN TO HIM, CRUZ!

YOU LOOK GOOD!

IT'S IMPORTANT TO LOOK THE PART. YOU CAN'T HAVE EVERYONE THINKING THAT YOU DON'T DESERVE TO BE HERE.

HE'S TRYING TO GET IN YOUR HEAD!

THEY DON'T NEED TO KNOW WHAT YOU AND I ALREADY DO...
...THAT YOU CAN PLAY DRESS UP ALL YOU WANT...
...BUT YOU'LL NEVER BE ONE OF US.

VVVMMM!

"CRUZ, DID YOU SEE WHAT HAPPENED THERE?"

YEAH. HE'S IN...HE'S IN MY HEAD...

NO. NO! LISTEN TO ME--YOU GOT INTO HIS HEAD. DON'T YOU UNDERSTAND? HE WOULD NEVER HAVE DONE THAT IF YOU DIDN'T SCARE HIM.
WHAT?

HE SEES SOMETHING IN YOU THAT YOU DON'T EVEN SEE IN YOURSELF. YOU MADE ME BELIEVE IT, BUT NOW YOU GOTTA BELIEVE IT, TOO.

YOU ARE A RACER.

HUH...

USE THAT.

VRRRR

AND HOW FAR BACK IS SHE NOW?
LOOK BEHIND YOU!
WHAT?!

GOOD EVENIN', STORM!

WHAT, HOW DID YOU--

JUST BACK HERE DRAFTING ON YOUR BUTT. NOTHING TO BE CONCERNED ABOUT.

JUST LIKE TWO JUNE BUGS ON A SUMMER NIGHT!

HA-HA-HAH!

HEY, HAMILTON...
HAMILTON HERE.
CALL OUT OUR SPEED.

208 MILES PER HOUR. 207 MILES PER HOUR--

WOULD YOU STOP THAT!
--205 MILES PER HOUR!
YOU'RE TAKIN' ME OFF MY LINE!
20
LAST LAP!

UH-OH. MY GPS IS SAYING I HAVE SLOW TRAFFIC IN MY WAY.
WVVRR!

YOU ARE NOT WINNING THIS!
VVVRRRRR!
AW, YOU'RE ANGRY.

I AM NOT ANGRY.
FINAL LAP
YOU KNOW, YOU CAN USE THAT ANGER TO PUSH THROUGH...
WWWVVVRRR!

I SAID I AM NOT ANGRY!!!
SLAM!

AAH!
OH, I DON'T THINK SO!
SKKKKRREE!

CRUZ! GET OUT OF THERE!

ERG...
YOU...
SKKKRREE!

...YOU DON'T BELONG ON THIS TRACK!!!
SKKKKRREE!
YES...

SKKKKRREE!
...I...
FINAL LAP
FINAL LAP

SKKKKRREE!
...DO!!!
FINAL LAP

FWIP!
FINAL LAP
FINAL LAP

FINAL LAP
FINAL LAP

GASP!

WWOOO!

THWUD!

VVRRRZZZZMMM!

"I DON'T BELIEVE IT! IT'S CRUZ RAMIREZ FOR THE WIN!!!"
"I AM SPEECHLESS!"
FINAL LAP
OOOOO-HOOO-HOO!

WAY TO GO, CRUZ!!!

OHHHH, YEEESS!
ONE WAY

WHU-HHUH-HHHUU...
WOO-HOO!
RADIATOR SPRINGS CURIOS

"MAN! HECKUVA WIN!"

YEAH. HECKUVA WIN.

HEY, CRUZ! YOU WERE FLYING!
THANKS!

YOU REALLY HAD IT ROLLING TODAY.

THAT WAS COOL.
THANK YOU.

HEY, CRUZ, YOUR BLINKER'S ON.
IT IS? OH, YOU GOT ME! VERY FUNNY!

CRUZ!
CRUZ!
CRUZ!

GO AHEAD, GIVE 'EM SOME SMOKE.

HA!
SKRREEE!

SKKKKRREE!

SKKKKRREEEE!

UUHH...

COUGH!
WHEEZE!

YOU'LL GET USED TO THAT.

OUT OF MY WAY! C'MON, MOVE IT! MOVE!

CRUUUZ, I *KNEW* YOU HAD SOMETHING--AND NOW LOOK AT YOU, A WINNER.

I COULD USE YOU AS A RACER ON OUR TEAM. WE COULD MAKE--

SORRY, MR. STERLING. I WOULD NEVER RACE FOR YOU. I QUIT.

honk!
honk!
WELL, THEN RACE FOR ME!

TEX!

MISS CRUZ, I WOULD BE TICKLED PINK TO HAVE YA RACE FOR TEAM DINOCO. AS YOU KNOW, WE HAVE A LONG HISTORY OF GREAT RACERS...'CEPT FOR CAL.

AH, GUYS, I'M STILL RIGHT HERE.

TEAM DINOCO, CRUZ!

HIRE HER, I DON'T CARE. LIGHTNING, NOW THAT YOU'RE RETIRED, I NEED YOU FIRST THING MONDAY MORNING FOR A PHOTO SHOOT.
24

YEAH, ALL RIGHT, MR. STERLING.

WHOA, HANG ON NOW.

WHAT? WHY IS MY NAME UP THERE?
GASP WHA--?
YOU STARTED THE RACE, THAT'S HOW IT WORKS...

WAIT, WAIT, NOW WAIT A MINUTE, NO--

UH, LIGHTNING WINS, HE DECIDES WHEN HE'S DONE RACING, THAT WAS THE DEAL. HI. I'M HIS LAWYER.

THAT WAS THE DEAL. YOU ARE NOT A NICE GUY--

--ALTHOUGH SERIOUSLY, I GOTTA SAY, YOU DO MAKE A QUALITY MUD FLAP AT AN AFFORDABLE PRICE.

AHEM HEY, STERLING! WHY DON'T YOU AND I TAKE A DRIVE AND TALK. BILLIONAIRE TO BILLIONAIRE.

CRUZ! OVER HERE! HOW DOES IT FEEL TO BEAT JACKSON STORM? TAKE US THROUGH IT, LAP BY LAP.

IT WAS GREAT! DIDN'T EXPECT THIS! THANK YOU!

KID'S GOT A LOT OF STUFF, EH, DOC?

WELL, SHE HAD A GREAT TEACHER.
AND, NOW YOU GET TO DECIDE WHEN YOU'RE DONE RACING. SO WHAT'S IT GONNA BE, STINKY-- UH, STICKERS?

OH, I'M GONNA KEEP RACING.

BUT BEFORE THAT, I GOT SOMETHIN' I WANNA DO.

WELCOME, ALL, TO HISTORIC WILLYS BUTTE FOR TODAY'S GREAT EXHIBITION OF SPEED!

NICE PAINT, KIDDO!

PARDON ME...BIG HAT, COMING THROUGH. GET 'ER DONE, "51"!
51

GREAT NUMBER.
WAS MCQUEEN'S IDEA.
HE FELT HUD WOULDA WANTED YA TO HAVE IT.
OH, IT'S PERFECT. IT'S IT'S *VERY* OLD SCHOOL.

I LOVE IT.

Rust-eze
HORNET
95
FOR DOC HUDSON
DID SOMEONE JUST SAY "OLD SCHOOL"?!

FABULOUS LIGHTNING
McQUEEN
LIGHTYEAR

DOC'S BACK FROM COLLEGE!
TRYIN' SOMETHIN' NEW. I LIKE IT.

WOW. SUBTLE.
DINOCO
DINOCO
51

FIGURED IF I'M GONNA BE YOUR CREW CHIEF, I BETTER DO IT IN STYLE.
YOU KNOW, I'M ACTUALLY MORE WORRIED ABOUT WHAT TEX IS GONNA SAY, CONSIDERING HE, UHHH, *BOUGHT* RUST-EZE.
WHAT'S MR. STERLING GOING TO SAY?
THANKS, TEX!

I MADE THAT STERLING FELLA A TEXAS-SIZED OFFER! YEE-HAW!
51

SO, YOU READY TO START TRAINING?

I DON'T KNOW. YOU READY TO LOSE AGAIN?

OH-HO-HO...HOPE YOU'VE GOT YOUR FLUFFY CLOUD.
HOPE YOU GOT YOUR DRIP PAN.

GOT MY DRIP PAN AND I'VE TAKEN MY NAP.
BRING IT ON, OLD MAN.

LUIGI?

WOO-HOO!
GO!!!
VRRRRZZZM!

VVVWWWRRMM!

WOOO!
GO!!!

THE END.

Directed by
Brian Fee

Produced by
Kevin Reher

Screenplay by
Robert L. Baird
Dan Gerson
Kiel Murray
Bob Peterson
Mike Rich

Story by
Brian Fee
Ben Queen
Eyal Podell
Jonathon E. Stewart